Praise for

Miranda AND MAUDE

"Brilliantly relevant, playful, and compassionate." —Abby Hanlon, author of *Dory Fantasmagory*

"This unlikely combination of royalty and social justice delivers fun, learning, and laughs." —*Kirkus Reviews*

"A totally delightful story guaranteed to please young readers." —*School Library Connection* written by

EMMA WUNSCH

illustrated by

JESSIKA VON INNEREBNER

Amulet Books
New York

Miranda AND MAUDE 1

THE PRINCESS AND THE Absolutely NOT a Princess

PUBLISHER'S NOTE: This is a work of fiction. Names, characters, places, and incidents are either the product of the author's imagination or used fictitiously, and any resemblance to actual persons, living or dead, business establishments, events, or locales is entirely coincidental.

Library of Congress Cataloging-in-Publication Data
Names: Wunsch, Emma, author. | Von Innerebner, Jessika, illustrator.
Title: The princess and the-absolutely-not-a-princess / by Emma Wunsch; Illustrated by Jessika von Innerebner.
Description: New York: Amulet Books, 2018. | Series: Miranda and Maude; volume 1 | Summary: Princess Miranda is horrified when her parents insist she attend public school, especially because Maude, who sits next to her in 3B, is everything the princess finds most offensive.
Identifiers: LCCN 2017052443 | ISBN 978-1-4197-3179-2 (hardcover POB)
Subjects: | CYAC: Schools—Fiction. | Princesses—Fiction. | Social action—Fiction. | Friendship—Fiction.
Classification: LCC PZ7.1.W97 Pri 2018 | DDC [E]—dc23

Paperback ISBN 978-1-4197-3374-1

Book design by Alyssa Nassner

Printed and bound in USA
10 9 8 7 6 5 4 3 2 1

ABRAMS The Art of Books
195 Broadway, New York, NY 10007
abramsbooks.com

THE MIRANDA AND MAUDE SERIES

Book One: *The Princess and the Absolutely Not a Princess*

Book Two: *Banana Pants!*

Book Three: *Girls Versus Boys*

1

PRINCESS MIRANDA DOES NOT WANT TO GO TO SCHOOL

It was Princess Miranda's first first day of school. She had never been to school before, and she absolutely, positively did not want to go.

But she was going!

Just one hour ago, her parents, the king and queen, had woken her up and said, "Time to go to school!"

At first, Miranda had thought she was dreaming. She was a princess! She lived in an enormous castle filled with fancy and expensive things. She didn't get woken up and told to go to school. She had a wonderful, very old royal tutor named Madame Cornelia who came at noon, napped at one, and left promptly at two.

But apparently, things had changed.

Because here she was. Curled up in the back of a fancy automobile being driven to school.

Miranda's mother, whom the princess called QM (which was short for Queen Mom), squeezed her daughter's hand.

"You might like it," QM whispered, as Blake, the driver of the fancy automobile, turned into a parking lot with a sign that said MOUNTAIN RIVER VALLEY ELEMENTARY SCHOOL.

The princess shook her head. She knew she would absolutely, positively hate school.

2

THE PRINCESS GETS OUT OF THE CAR

As soon as the royal automobile stopped, a tall man with a long, curling mustache ran over.

"HOW DO YOU DO?" the tall man boomed. "I'M PRINCIPAL FISH!" He clutched a very thick book against the middle of his chest.

"Lovely to meet you," QM said. She looked at Miranda, who was looking at her feet and wondering what would happen to her fancy shoes. Miranda had a feeling that school was full of dirt and sand and glue, all of which could ruin her beautiful shoes.

"HERE'S A COPY OF THE *OFFICIAL RULES OF MOUNTAIN RIVER VALLEY ELEMENTARY.*

IT HAS EVERY SINGLE RULE OF THE SCHOOL. IT'S VERY USEFUL," Principal Fish yelled, holding out the thick book.

"Thank you," replied QM.

"AND NOW I'LL TAKE YOU TO MEET YOUR TEACHER," hollered Principal Fish. "NORMALLY STUDENTS ARE NOT ALLOWED IN UNTIL SEVEN FORTY-TWO, BUT BECAUSE YOU'RE NEW, YOU'RE NOT BREAKING RULE NUMBER FORTY-SIX!"

If Princess Miranda noticed how loudly Principal Fish spoke, she didn't show it. Still looking down at her shoes, she followed QM and Principal Fish inside Mountain River Valley Elementary, which smelled revoltingly like hard-boiled eggs, which the princess despised. As soon as she was old enough to speak, she had forbidden hard-boiled eggs inside the castle.

The princess held her breath as Principal Fish walked them past the gymnasium (which smelled like socks), his office (which smelled like onions and old fish), and the library (which smelled like joy and cinnamon). He took a left at the cafeteria and walked down the hall, until he reached a room with a sign on the door that said 3B in bright yellow letters.

"THREE B!" Principal Fish shouted. "MIRANDA, THIS IS YOUR CLASSROOM!"

"And I'll be your teacher," a young woman with brown hair said from the doorway. "I'm Miss Kinde. That's kind with an *e*." Her voice was soothing and quiet.

Miranda looked confused.

"She's not a great speller," QM said. "She's probably behind in math and science, too. Her royal tutor . . ." QM wasn't quite sure how to explain Madame Cornelia to Miss Kinde, so she looked at her daughter, who wasn't listening to her, because she was still looking down.

Shoes this nice, the princess was thinking, *should not be in school*. The shoes, which were heeled, pink, and sparkly, were meant to be on ballroom floors or red carpets, not in hallways that smelled like hard-boiled eggs!

"YOU'RE IN GREAT HANDS WITH MISS KINDE!" Principal Fish roared. "BUT I MUST GO NOW. THE CHILDREN ARE COMING!" He took off, practically (but not quite) running. Running broke rule number two in the *Official Rules of Mountain River Valley Elementary*.

"Let me show you and your mom around, Miranda," Miss Kinde said kindly but firmly.

Miranda finally looked up from her feet and walked into the classroom, which, thankfully, didn't smell like anything. QM followed behind her.

"We're going to have a great year," Miss Kinde said. "You're going to love Three B."

Miranda stared at the woman in front of her. She'd never *like* 3B, let alone love it! As Miss Kinde talked about book nooks and science centers, the princess's head began to ache. She glanced out the window at the empty playground. She'd probably have to go out there, she thought, her stomach somersaulting.

Even though Miranda was a kid, she did not enjoy kid things, like monkey bars or ice pops or freeze tag. She liked nail polish, shoes, shoe shopping, arranging furniture, clothes, clothes shopping, rearranging furniture, and planning parties. She also liked being quiet.

Miranda had been perfectly happy with Madame Cornelia, who had been the royal tutor for around a century. Madame Cornelia often forgot to teach things like math or spelling or science. She loved to talk about china patterns and antiques and never noticed if Miranda got up to paint her nails or take a bubble bath during their lessons, which were often about china patterns and antiques. But now Madame Cornelia had decided to retire (to focus on her antique china patterns)!

Miranda knew that soon the empty, quiet playground would fill up with children who would scream and shout. Miranda did not spend much time with children and/or playgrounds, and she didn't want to.

Miranda looked at her mother, but QM was too busy listening to Miss Kinde to notice. The princess rubbed her head and looked out the window again. Just as she had feared, millions of children wearing bright and clashing color combinations were streaming toward the playground. The children wore polka dots, stripes, and plaids and arrived by foot, scooters, and cars. They came by bike and bus. Some little ones cried and tried to hide, while the bigger ones zoomed in, shouting at friends.

Friends, the princess thought with a shudder. She'd never have anything to talk about with kids her age. What if they wanted her to do something terrible with them like playing tag or climbing on top of the monkey bars? The princess gulped a mouthful of air.

Miranda watched as Principal Fish walked to the middle of the playground hugging an over-sized clipboard to his chest. When the children on the playground saw him, they scrambled into many crooked lines.

Head and heart and stomach pounding, Miranda looked away from the playground and

over to her teacher. Miss Kinde smiled. "You can take your seat now," she said, pointing to a desk in the back left of the classroom that had a name tag on it that said *Miranda Rose Lapointsetta*. QM walked over to the princess, kissed her on the head, and told her to have a wonderful day.

An extremely loud bell rang out at a terrifying volume. Princess Miranda's heart sank as she dropped into the seat and watched her mother walk away. The princess had never been to school before, but she knew that at any minute a group of loud children would come into the classroom and want to know what in the world she was doing there.

3

MAUDE BRANDYWINE MAYHEW KAYE IS SO HAPPY SHE'S NOT LATE

While Miranda sat frozen at her desk inside 3B, Miss Kinde stepped back into the hard-boiled-eggs-smelling hallway to greet her students. As each child walked inside the classroom, Miss Kinde looked them in the eye, smiled, and said, "Welcome to Three B. Please find your desk and take a seat." Miss Kinde had a lovely, honey-like voice, so it was pleasant to hear her say this fifteen times.

The last person to be greeted by Miss Kinde was out of breath, freckled, and wearing huge rectangular glasses on top of her head and roller skates over her shoes. She was also the only person who shook Miss Kinde's hand and stopped to chat.

"Hello," the girl said, taking a big gulp of air. "My name is Maude Brandywine Mayhew Kaye. I'm so happy I'm not late on the first day! I can't believe I slept through my rooster!"

Miss Kinde gave the girl a small smile.

"My rooster, General Cockatoo, is my alarm clock. I have ten chickens. Actually eleven. I got a new one last week. Her name is Rosalie, and she's my only Frizzle. She has curly feathers!"

Miss Kinde nodded. "Welcome to Three B, Maude."

"I feel most welcome. Miss Creaky taught me nothing last year," Maude said, pointing down the hall to last year's classroom. "She's probably one hundred and two years old." Maude moved her glasses from her head to her eyes.

Miss Kinde glanced inside 3B. The class was getting noisy, but Maude wasn't done talking.

"I want you to know that I choose to come to school, Miss Kinde. Every year my dad, Walter

Matthews Mayhew Kaye the eighth, asks me and Michael-John, that's my brother, how we plan to learn. I always choose school!"

Miss Kinde smiled.

"Michael-John chooses home school. He stays in his pajamas and reads dictionaries. He knows practically every word. But I want to be a social justice advocate when I grow up. That's someone who makes sure things are equal for all people. So I need to be with The People! I thought about being a farmer, but I had a terrible time with my tomato plant this summer." Maude sighed. "The plant grew and grew, but I didn't get one tomato."

"Tomatoes need lots of sun," Miss Kinde said, shifting on her feet.

"I gave it lots of sunshine!" Maude pushed the glasses back on top of her head and tried to sound passionate and sincere.

"Perhaps we'll study tomatoes," Miss Kinde said. "Now please find your desk and remove your skates. You know they're not allowed in school."

"Rule fifty-eight," Maude recited proudly. "No wearing wheeled shoes on school grounds." She whistled as she skated over to her desk, which was in the back left corner of the room. Maude sat down, removed her skates, and took out a hard-boiled egg and five pencils from the big pockets of her pants. She put everything on her desk in a jumble and waited for something interesting to happen.

When nothing happened, Maude looked around and sighed. Here were all the same kids she'd gone to school with for around three hundred years. None of her classmates had taken their seats yet or asked how her summer had been. Like usual, Agnes and Agatha were giggling. Desdemona was chatting with Norbert, while Fletcher showed Felix his scabby elbow. Over by the Book Nook, a tall boy named Donut was seeing how long he could balance on one leg. Maude's heart sank as she watched the dreadful Hillary Greenlight-Miller put an apple on Miss Kinde's desk.

Hillary Greenlight-Miller had gotten glasses over the summer. Glasses that weren't enormous and seemed to stay on her eyes. Maude put her glasses on her desk and looked at them wistfully. She was only able to wear them for ten seconds at a time. Any longer and she'd feel dizzy, like she might throw up. For years, Maude had wished with all her might that she would need glasses, since all the best social justice revolutionaries wore them. Unfortunately, despite getting many opinions, Maude still had perfect vision. Although she'd missed something right next to her that everyone else in the class had definitely seen.

In addition to hugging and chatting, the other students in 3B were staring at the girl in the left corner of the room who was not Maude. Fletcher, Felix, Desdemona, Norbert, and Hillary Greenlight-Miller, along with everyone else, couldn't help but stare at Princess Miranda. They couldn't believe an actual princess was just sitting there!

Maude and Miss Kinde were the only two people in 3B not buzzing from the excitement of having a princess in class. Miss Kinde loved all children, and Maude, who was busy straightening her wobbly hard-boiled egg, hadn't looked to her right yet.

4

MAUDE LOOKS TO HER RIGHT

When the final morning bell rang, a fly landed on Maude's wrist. She flicked the fly off, causing her to look to her right, and that's when she noticed: Someone was next to her! Someone new! And this new someone, like Maude, was sitting!

Keeping one hand on her wobbly egg, Maude put on her glasses and glanced at the new girl again. How did she know that face?

Miss Kinde stepped to the front of the room. "Class! Let's begin. I'm Miss Kinde—that's kind with a silent *e*. We're going to have a terrific year. First, let's welcome our new classmate. Miranda, welcome to Mountain River Valley. Welcome to Three B."

Maude's glasses slid straight down her nose. *Princess* Miranda? She was sitting next to a princess? No wonder she looked familiar! All her life, Maude had seen pictures and heard stories about the royal family. Whenever they drove by the castle, Maude's dad would dream aloud about all the undiscovered beetles on the property. To Maude Brandywine Mayhew Kaye, Princess Miranda had always seemed like a character in a book, not an actual person. And yet here she was, right next to Maude, just thirteen inches away!

This was an opportunity, Maude thought. Here, finally, was another girl who looked as out of place as Maude felt, even though Maude had been going to Mountain River Valley for around nine million years.

Maude had to seize this opportunity! She looked at the princess. She looked at her egg.

"Would you like a hard-boiled egg?" she asked.

The princess didn't say anything.

Maybe she didn't hear me, Maude thought. She picked up her egg. "Would you like this egg?" she asked a little louder, nudging the egg closer to the princess. "It comes from my chickens," she said proudly. "I have eleven chickens. And one rooster named General Cockatoo. That's a funny name, because cockatoos are parrots, not chickens." Maude laughed.

The princess remained quiet and wrinkled her nose.

"I love all animals. But chickens are my favorite. Well, second favorite. My dog, Rudolph Valentino, is the most amazing dog in the universe. But he doesn't lay eggs." Maude laughed again. It would be so great if her dog could lay eggs!

The princess finally turned to look at Maude. Maude grinned as widely as she could.

"Would you like this egg?" Maude asked again.

"No!" the princess said. Her voice wasn't loud, but it was very clear. "Hard-boiled eggs are . . ."

Maude stared at the princess. She hoped the princess might say something like, "Hard-boiled eggs are too delicious to have in school. Why don't we eat them together in the castle, and you can tell me all about your amazing chickens?"

But instead the princess whispered, "Hard-boiled eggs are revolting! They make me want to vomit!"

5

YOU JOURNALS

Maude felt small and weak when Miranda said her egg was revolting. She glared at the princess, who was wearing all pink. *I hate pink*, she thought, as Miss Kinde held up a small blue notebook. *Pink is the worst color in the universe.*

"Class," Miss Kinde said, "this is a You Journal. It's a notebook that's just for you. It should be with you at all times, because you never know when you'll have an amazing idea."

Everyone in 3B groaned except Maude (who loved the idea of a notebook for amazing ideas) and Miranda (who was confused).

Hillary Greenlight-Miller shot up her hand. "Miss Kinde? Will our You Journals be graded? If we write a lot, can we get extra credit?"

Miss Kinde shook her head. "Your You Journals are only for you. No one else should read them."

Hillary Greenlight-Miller frowned, but everyone else seemed pleased. Maude opened her You Journal and immediately drew the following:

Then she drew this:

6

TOTALLY ALONE AT STICKY DESK

Princess Miranda had stopped breathing. Through her nose, that is. She was trying to breathe only with her mouth so she wouldn't have to smell the hideous egg. The owner of the disgusting egg kept putting on and taking off a pair of ugly glasses and was busily writing in her You Journal.

Miranda didn't know what she was supposed to write in the journal. She didn't understand anything Miss Kinde had said. Plus, she didn't have a pencil. But even if she did have a pencil, she wouldn't have known what to write. She hated writing. And reading. And school. And hard-boiled eggs! She felt alone and stared at. Every few minutes, someone else in 3B turned around to look at her.

Miranda didn't mind being stared at when

she walked down a red carpet between QM and KD (King Dad). Safe between her parents, she was happy to give a little wave and a smile. But being stared at in school felt different. In a bad way. The princess felt all alone at her slightly sticky desk and chair.

She looked up at the clock on the wall and was filled with dread. The clock hadn't moved at all! She'd be here for another six and a half hours. Miranda didn't think her first day of school would ever end.

She missed Madame Cornelia and desperately wished something terrible would happen that would let her skip school for the rest of her life (but not something too terrible that would ruin her shoes). She closed her eyes, rubbed her temples, and sniffed. The horrible egg smell was making her headache even worse.

She had known that school would be full of noisy children. She had known that there would be teachers and tests. But she hadn't realized that the grossest food in the universe would be right next to her! *Everyone* knew Miranda hated hard-boiled eggs. How could she be sitting right next to one? Didn't the girl next to her know who she was?

The princess tried not to breathe, but the hard-boiled-egg smell was getting stronger.

Finally, after several centuries passed, a bell rang, and Miranda and the rest of 3B left the classroom and went to a horrible smelly place where they were told to eat. But Miranda couldn't eat, even though the castle chef had packed her favorite cheeses, along with fresh croissants and fruit.

After that, 3B went to another loud and smelly room where a woman laughed as she hurled balls over some kind of net. Finally, 3B went back to 3B, where Miss Kinde told them a million things about after-school clubs, and then about three million rules were announced over the loudspeaker. Then, finally-finally, the dismissal bell rang.

Miranda dragged her aching feet and head down the long hallway, out of school, and over to the carpool lane, where Blake had parked the fancy automobile.

"That goes against rule number forty-nine," she heard a voice call from above.

The princess looked up and saw the hard-boiled-egg girl sitting in a tree.

"According to the *Official Rules of Mountain River Valley Elementary,* cars can't *park* in the carpool lane. And they can't pick up one child."

Miranda ignored Maude and crawled into the back seat of the royal automobile.

She had done it.

She'd gone to school for an entire day.

She only hoped she wouldn't have to do it ever again.

7

UP A TREE

Even though it went against rule number ninety-seven, Maude was sitting up in the oak tree in front of school. Principal Fish was so busy dealing with students who had broken first day rules (running, chewing gum, spitting, running while chewing gum and spitting) that she figured she'd get away with it.

It was a sunny afternoon, and Maude was happy to be outside, but she was getting hungry watching the jump-roping club eat ice pops over in the playground. Behind them, the gardening club munched veggies. Maude took out a small pair of binoculars from her pants and focused them on the gardening club's tomato plants. There were lots of tomatoes growing on the vines.

No fair, she thought. *Why didn't my plant grow tomatoes?* She would have liked to ask the gardening club gardeners, but Hillary Greenlight-Miller was president, and Maude didn't spend any more time with Hillary than she had to. How annoying that Hillary got to wear glasses and eat homegrown tomatoes even though she didn't really like gardening. Hillary just liked being president, which was why, in addition to the gardening club, she was president of the marbles club, the yo-yo club, the homework club, and the practice Mandatory National Reading and Writing and Math Exam club, of which she was the only member. Maude wasn't in any clubs, because Hillary was in all of them.

But still, Maude thought, even with her arch-nemesis Hillary Greenlight-Miller, 3B seemed much better than 2L. When Maude got home, she'd tell her dad and brother just that. Then her brother would define a word she didn't know, and her dad would ask her if she'd learned anything. Maude closed her eyes in thought. Miss Kinde was nice, and she really liked her You Journal, but Maude couldn't think of anything she'd learned. Her classmates still weren't interested in anything she liked, and not one of them had asked her what she'd done over summer vacation.

Her stomach growled. *I learned that one hard-boiled egg isn't nearly enough lunch*, she thought. Then Maude remembered how Princess Miranda had said hard-boiled eggs were revolting. Maude opened her eyes. She *had* learned something! She'd learned that princesses were rude!

Rudeness was a kind of injustice, Maude thought. Rudeness shouldn't be tolerated! Feeling

motivated, Maude packed up her binoculars, swung herself out of the tree, and roller-skated home in a record-breaking six minutes.

When Maude got home, she took off her skates, climbed up twenty-seven slightly crooked stairs, and burst into her house. "You're never going to believe it!" she called.

"I always believe you, Maude," her dad said. Her dad, Walter Matthews Mayhew Kaye VIII, was doing a headstand, as he'd been when she'd left him that morning. Maude's dad had many interests, including yoga, beetles, juggling, soup making, and reciting quotes to his children every morning.

Maude's brother, Michael-John, was also where she'd left him, which was in sheep pajamas, hunched over a stack of dictionaries.

"There's a princess in my class this year," Maude announced, petting Rudolph Valentino, her beloved dog.

Walt lowered his left leg, Michael-John turned to page 802 in a musty dictionary, and Rudolph Valentino yawned, then farted.

"Do you want a snack, my little mountain pine beetle? There's some cheese on the counter."

Maude looked at her father and then her brother, who was still reading. "Did you hear me say there's a princess in my class? An actual, real-life princess. She sits next to me since we're in alphabetical order."

"I heard you." Walt lowered his right leg. "William Shakespeare wrote, 'My crown is in my heart, not on my head.' Does your princess wear a crown?" He flipped so he was suddenly sitting cross-legged in front of Maude.

"She's not *my* princess," Maude told him. "And no, she wasn't wearing a crown. Just loads of pink, which I learned is the worst color in the world."

Walt smiled. "That's a matter of opinion. I like pink. So, my coconut rhinoceros beetle, have you and the real-life pink princess become friends?"

Maude stared at her father. For someone who knew so much about so many things, he was totally bananas. "No," she said. "I have absolutely, positively *not* become friends with the princess." *And I never will*, she thought.

8

WHEN MIRANDA GOT HOME

When Miranda slowly walked into the castle, QM and KD were waiting in the entryway.

"How was the first day, darling?" QM asked eagerly.

"What did you learn?" KD asked. "Tell me one thing."

"Did you make friends? Is your teacher nice?" QM asked.

"Did you have enough to eat?" KD smiled at her.

Staring at her parents in their fancy clothes, Miranda realized there were not enough words in her vocabulary to describe her first day of school. How could she explain all the rules? Or how often and loudly the bells rang? What about the way the children in 3B stared at her? And, perhaps most strange of all, how she, Princess Miranda, known hater of hard-boiled eggs, had been offered a hard-boiled egg! How could she explain all this?

"There . . ." Miranda choked out. "There was . . ."

QM and KD smiled eagerly.

"THERE WAS A HARD-BOILED EGG!" Miranda shouted. Then she ran past her parents, through several long hallways, and up several spiraling staircases, before entering her wing and collapsing on her enormous, perfectly made bed.

The princess stayed in bed for the rest of the day. And the night. She wished, more than anything, that she could stay there forever. Unfortunately, just after sunrise, her parents rushed in.

"Good morning, sunshine!" QM beamed.

"It's the second day of school!" KD shouted happily.

"I can't get up," the princess said. Even though she'd been in bed for many hours, she hadn't slept and felt tired. And miserable.

"Of course you can get out of bed," KD said cheerfully.

The princess shook her head. "I'm sick."

QM put her hand on her daughter's forehead.

"It's my stomach," the princess said. "And my head."

"You're going to school, Miranda," KD told her.

"Can't Madame Cornelia come back?" Miranda begged. "She could give me homework."

"No," QM said. "Madame Cornelia finally retired. She's not coming back."

The princess scowled.

"Your father and I have come to believe that school is better than having a royal tutor come here." QM looked at all the fabulous things in her daughter's room. There was the Victorian doll-house that was big enough for Miranda to stand in, a hammock suspended from the ceiling, a ninety-inch pink television set, and a wall of very organized nail polishes. "It's good for you to spend time out of the castle with people your own age."

Miranda rolled onto her side and looked at the pink wall. People her age? People her age didn't know the difference between the color char-treuse and the color cerulean! If her endless first day of school had taught her anything, it was that people her age wore ugly shoes, chewed gum, and talked with their mouths full.

Not that they talked to her. They just stared at her and then whispered and giggled. Normally, being a princess made Miranda feel different in a special way, but yesterday she had just felt dif-ferent in a weird way. Why didn't anyone else jump when the loud bells rang? What was the Mandatory National Reading and Writing and Math Exam, and why did everyone in 3B groan every time Miss Kinde mentioned it? She didn't understand what the kids talked about either. What was an allowance? And why on earth would anyone have a pet chicken?

Chickens, the princess thought with a shudder. Chickens laid eggs! Spending time with people her age meant spending time with people like the hard-boiled-egg girl!

"I can't go to school," she moaned.

"Of course you can," said KD. "Why couldn't you?"

"It smells," the princess said. "And it gives me a terrible headache."

QM lifted the pink blanket off of the princess.

"Up and at 'em, Miranda," KD commanded. "You're going back to school."

9

MIRANDA GOES BACK TO SCHOOL

The second day at Mountain River Valley began with an assembly, during which experts expertly explained the best way for students to bubble in the green answer sheets for the practice Mandatory National Reading and Writing and Math Exams they would take all year.

For everyone except Hillary Greenlight-Miller, the assembly, like the exam, was painful and boring. Princess Miranda did not understand a word, and Maude spent most of the time looking for her You Journal in her messy messenger bag. When she finally found it, she doodled this:

After the assembly, 3B walked back to 3B, which was stuffy and warm. Miss Kinde passed out long sheets of green paper and thick test booklets and opened the classroom windows. Miranda was grateful for the fresh air, but then Maude put three pencils, a long feather, and *two* hard-boiled eggs on her desk!

Miranda gasped.

Miss Kinde, thinking the princess was concerned about the test, ran over. "This is a Mandatory National Reading and Writing and Math Exam," she explained.

The princess rubbed her aching head.

"Don't worry," her teacher said. "It's only a practice test. You'll take many practice exams." She sighed as if this made her very sad. "The real exam is at the end of the year."

The princess nodded, although she knew she wouldn't make it to the end of her second *day*, let alone the end of the *year*.

"Just do as well as you can," Miss Kinde added.

"I don't have a pencil," the princess said quietly.

"Oh." Miss Kinde looked around, her eyes stopping on Maude. "Maude, may Miranda borrow a pencil?"

Maude scowled but handed one to the princess.

"You may begin, class," Miss Kinde said.

While 3B bubbled in their ovals, the classroom lights flickered, and Miranda's head pounded. Just reading the questions made her so tired and weak that she could barely hold Maude's terrible pencil. The point was so dull that Miranda had to use all the energy in her hand to fill an oval. And she soon discovered that the pencil had barely any eraser, so when she tried to erase answer three, the sheet ripped.

Then a gentle breeze breezed into 3B and swept the hard-boiled-egg smell right into Miranda's nose. She closed her eyes. Two hard-boiled eggs were so much smellier than one.

The princess opened her eyes and glanced at the hard-boiled-egg girl. Maude's test booklet was closed, and she was writing in her You Journal.

Miranda's heart sank. How could Maude be

done already? Miranda had about eight hundred more questions to bubble in. And what was Maude writing? Miranda hadn't written a single word in her stupid You Journal.

Another breeze forced so much hard-boiled-egg smell into the princess's nose that she sneezed, very loudly, three times in a row. The class turned to look at her. She sneezed again, and her eyes began to water. She couldn't hate hard-boiled eggs any more!

Something orange landed on her desk. The princess stared at it. She was afraid to touch it because it was covered with sticky bits and some kind of fur.

"It's a handkerchief," Maude whispered. "You can use it."

Miranda shook her head, which made her nose drip.

"You don't want my handkerchief?" Maude hissed.

"No," the princess muttered. She thought of her collection of handkerchiefs back in the castle. They were clean, and silk, and, thanks to Madame Cornelia's instruction, folded into perfect triangles! Now *those* were handkerchiefs!

"Your nose is dripping, but you won't use my handkerchief, even though it was in the famous War of Jenkin's Ear?"

"Class, you have three minutes left," Miss Kinde announced.

Three minutes, the princess thought. *Three minutes to get through eight hundred questions.*

"Are you too good to use my handkerchief?" Maude whispered.

What does good have to do with it? Miranda wondered. She just wanted to be left alone in her wing of the castle for the rest of her life. The princess closed her eyes and pictured her beautiful, quiet room. She missed her shoes, her closets, and all of her nail polishes. She missed all the time she used to have to organize her things and arrange her furniture. She sneezed again. And again. And again. If only she'd brought a real handkerchief! And a gallon of perfume.

"Do you think you're better than me because I'm just a humble social justice activist?" Maude asked.

Miranda didn't understand Maude's question or any of the questions on the practice exam. She didn't know why someone would put hard-boiled eggs on their desk or get mad when someone else didn't want to use a filthy bandana.

"One minute remaining," Miss Kinde said sweetly.

Except for Maude and Miranda, all the other kids in 3B quickly finished filling in their ovals. Tears welled in the princess's eyes as she looked at her nearly blank answer sheet. She had no answers.

"Well?" Maude asked.

"It smells," Miranda said finally. "The bandana

smells and so do your rotten eggs! Isn't there a rule about hard-boiled eggs in school?"

"No!" Maude said. "There is no rule about eggs!" With that, she grabbed her handkerchief and stuffed it into her pocket.

Princess Miranda breathed a small sigh of relief. Then she looked down at her practice Mandatory National Reading and Writing and Math Exam and felt miserable all over again.

10

DAY THREE AT MOUNTAIN RIVER VALLEY ELEMENTARY

Maude (who had stayed up late reading about growing tomatoes) and Miranda (who couldn't fall asleep on school nights) were both tired on the third day of school. But that was the only similar thing.

Maude wore an orange shirt that said FIGHT THE POWER, her dirty brown cargo pants, two different colored socks, and combat boots.

Miranda wore gold wedge shoes and a very shiny pink pantsuit.

When the bell rang, Maude (who had overslept again) rushed to her desk and set out her You Journal, three hard-boiled eggs, her harmonica, and five pencils.

Miranda put some things on her desk, too. She still hadn't found a pencil, but she'd brought a small pink candle, a diamond box of tissues, and a doily to cover her desk. She lined everything up in a very neat row.

"You can't light that candle," Maude told her. "It breaks rule seventy-seven. No burning sticks, leaves, homework, metal, or *candles* on school grounds."

"I'm not going to burn it," Miranda said quietly. "I just smell it." She picked the candle up and breathed in the sweet smell of "violets in the rain." If she kept her nose on the candle and closed her eyes, she could almost pretend she didn't smell the revolting hard-boiled eggs.

11

DAY FOUR AT MOUNTAIN RIVER VALLEY ELEMENTARY

On the fourth day at Mountain River Valley, Maude brought in four hard-boiled eggs, her orange handkerchief, a rusty harmonica, a set of yellow false teeth, a snakeskin, and a miniature ship in a bottle.

Miranda brought in her doily, two pink candles, the tissues in the diamond box, and a small bottle of nail polish called "pinktastically pink."

12

FRIDAY AT MOUNTAIN RIVER VALLEY ELEMENTARY

On the fifth day of school, Maude put a piece of blue cheese, eight pencils, the rusty harmonica, the orange handkerchief, the false teeth, and the snakeskin on her desk. There was so much stuff, the desk was barely visible, but then she reached into her green canvas bag and took out *six* hard-boiled eggs! She lined them up in a crooked row.

Next to her, Miranda reached into her fancy leather bag and set up, in neat rows, three candles, the doily, a small oval mirror, four bottles of nail polish, and a shiny ruby pen, because she still couldn't find a pencil anywhere in the castle.

It was the pen that brought everything to an end.

It was so shiny and sparkly that everyone in 3B, even Miss Kinde, kept looking at it.

"That is a lovely pen, Miranda," Miss Kinde said right before giving out yet another practice Mandatory National Reading and Writing and Math Exam. "But very distracting."

"Hard-boiled eggs are distracting, too," Miranda whispered, because she wasn't used to talking in class.

"Excuse me?" Miss Kinde said.

The princess felt too shy to repeat what she had said, but Hillary Greenlight-Miller, who had amazing hearing, yelled, "She said, 'Hard-boiled eggs are distracting, too,' Miss Kinde!"

In one second, thirty eyes were on Maude.

Maude scrunched her face. *There's nothing wrong with hard-boiled eggs*, she told herself. There was no rule against them!

"Maude?" Miss Kinde walked over to Maude's

desk. "Why do you have six hard-boiled eggs on your desk?"

"They're from my amazing chickens," Maude said, trying to sound proud. "I collect their eggs every morning. After I sing to them. There's no rule in the *Official Rules of Mountain River Valley Elementary* about hard-boiled eggs!"

Miss Kinde looked at Maude and her eggs, then at Miranda, then back at Maude's eggs. Finally, she said, "No, there's no rule against having hard-boiled eggs in school, but since lunch isn't for several hours, please put your eggs in your lunch bag."

"Maude always eats gross food," Hillary Greenlight-Miller announced.

"School lunches are grosser," Maude said to Hillary Greenlight-Miller.

Miranda couldn't help but nod as she watched Maude and Hillary stick their tongues out at each other. School lunches looked absolutely disgusting. It was all she could do to choke down a few bites of her own lunch, since the cafeteria smelled almost as bad as the gym and was as loud as the music room.

"Girls," Miss Kinde said, "there'll be no more discussion of lunch. Maude, put your eggs away."

"Do I have to? It's not in the *Official*—"

"It's a *class* rule," Miss Kinde said quickly. "Put the harmonica away, too. And the snakeskin, the cheese, and false teeth. You don't want distractions while taking the practice Mandatory National Reading and Writing and Math Exam."

"I'm not distracted," Maude grumbled, putting her things back in her bag. "I always get the highest score on the practice Mandatory National Reading and Writing and Math Exam."

She looked right at Hillary Greenlight-Miller, who stuck her tongue back out.

Princess Miranda sneezed and took one of the tissues out of the diamond box.

Maude pointed to the princess. "How come *she* gets to have stuff on her desk? Because she's a princess?"

It felt strange to hear Maude call her a princess, Miranda thought. Until that moment she wasn't sure Maude actually knew she was royal. Who would offer a princess a dirty handkerchief, dull pencils, or hard-boiled eggs?

Miss Kinde looked at all the things that were lined up on Miranda's desk. Then she cleared her throat. "Class," she said, "starting today, all personal items will be kept in your backpacks."

"Maude doesn't have a backpack," Hillary Greenlight-Miller said. "Just her ugly green sack."

"Hey!" Maude scowled at Hillary. "That bag belonged to my great-great-great-grandfather. With only eighteen cents and a one-eyed cat named Onion the Great, he explored the world on a unicycle!"

"Ewww," Hillary said. "One-eyed cats are the worst."

Maude scowled at Hillary. "My cat, Onion the Great Number Eleven, is lovely! But not as lovely as Rudolph Valentino, my dog."

"Animals belong in zoos," Hillary Greenlight-Miller said, straightening her glasses.

Maude gasped.

"Girls!" Miss Kinde said sharply. "Please, we must start the practice exam."

I don't have a backpack either, Miranda thought as she put her wonderful pen and candles and tissues in her fancy leather bag.

As Miss Kinde handed out the green paper with all the ovals, Maude glared at Miranda. "This is your fault," she said.

"What did I do?" Miranda whispered. "Miss Kinde made a new rule."

Maude looked at the princess. It was that sparkly pen that had caused her eggs and snakeskin and harmonica to be banned. *It wasn't fair,* she thought. *Why should Miranda and her stupid pen have so much power?*

13

BREAKFAST WITH KD AND QM

On Monday morning, the princess was miserable and tired. She'd spent the weekend trying to forget Mountain River Valley Elementary by rearranging a bunch of toys she didn't play with anymore and painting her toenails a dozen different times. But now it was the beginning of the week all over again, and she couldn't stop yawning as she ate her breakfast.

QM leaned across the long table and said, "Why Miranda, your birthday is just two weeks away!"

KD sat upright. "My mashed potatoes! How did we not remember?"

"Miranda has been busy." QM sounded pleased.

Miranda swallowed. Her birthday was in two weeks? She couldn't believe it! All the time she was wasting in school when she could have been party planning! Miranda always threw fantastic birthday parties and, until now, she'd always planned them weeks in advance. School was really getting in the way of all the things she liked to do.

"We'll pull out all the stops," KD said, "since this year's party will be different."

Princess Miranda looked at her dad. Her birthday parties were always incredible. Last year's party included a rocket launch, hot-air balloon rides, and a famous mariachi band. One year, there was a dolphin show. Every year, at the end of the party, fireworks spelled out HAPPY BIRTHDAY, MIRANDA! in bright pink explosions. Why would this year be different?

"This year," KD boomed, "Three B will be here!"

Miranda stared at her father.

"Why bother with the royal children of our royal friends when you have your very own classmates?" KD smiled at his excellent idea. Because Miranda didn't have any friends her age, the guests at her birthday parties had always been the children of the royal people QM and KD knew. Miranda never knew the tiny earls or teen-age dukes at her parties, but she didn't care. She just liked the planning part anyway.

"What a lovely way to meet Three B!" QM said.

"No," the princess said.

Her parents stared at her, which reminded her of all the staring the kids in 3B would be doing in school later that morning. "I can't invite Three B to my party," she told them.

"Why not?" KD asked.

Miranda looked up at the diamond chandelier above her. It was the perfect chandelier for the room, and she had chosen it because she was good at things like that. She understood how lights and tables should look in a room this big. Her parents didn't understand things like that and they wouldn't understand anything about 3B—certainly not how, just after Miss Kinde had said the new rule about how all home things had to be left in bags, the boy two seats in front of her, Fletcher, had asked for a pencil. He was talking to Maude, but since he was staring at Miranda, she accidentally handed him the ruby pen from her bag. Fletcher said something about pens on practice exams breaking rule number forty-two, which made her realize that the pen wasn't even supposed to be out of her bag! In a panic, she'd grabbed it, only to watch Maude hand Fletcher one of her sticky pencils.

Later, at recess, which was noisier than PE and lunch and music combined, Agatha had said she liked Miranda's sweater.

The princess had nodded.

"I love it!" Agatha had said, stepping closer to touch it. "Did you get it at Tops and Tees?"

Miranda shook her head.

"Pants and Pullovers?" Agatha asked.

Miranda had never heard of Tops and Tees or Pants and Pullovers, but she guessed they were clothing stores. She shook her head, hoping Agatha would go back to chasing Donut around the playground, but Agatha had stayed put.

"Where did you get it? I'd love one!"

Miranda didn't know how to tell Agatha about Yoshi von Mutter, the world-famous fashion designer, and his assistant tailor Starbella Loon. Four times a year, Yoshi and Starbella came to the castle to outfit the royal family for the upcoming season. For nearly a week, Miranda and Yoshi pored over magazines and swaths of the fanciest French fabrics. Yoshi would stay up every night cutting and trimming and measuring and sticking all kinds of pins in all kinds of places. At the end of the week, the royal family had exquisite one-of-a-kind wardrobes, and Yoshi and Starbella would jet off to their next royal family.

How could Miranda describe all this to Agatha? "I don't know . . ." she'd finally said. "It was in one of my closets."

Agatha had given her a weird look and walked away.

"Your class would love to come to your birthday party," QM said, jolting Miranda back to the breakfast table.

"No, they wouldn't," Miranda whispered.

"Of course they would." KD chuckled. "We'll borrow a lion! A white lion! Won't that be something?"

"I don't think they'd like it," Miranda said. "I don't think Three B will want to come to my party."

KD and QM laughed. "It's your birthday party!" KD said. "At our castle! What could they possibly not like?"

Me, Miranda thought. *They could not like me.*

14

THE INVITATIONS

But in the same way they'd decided that she was going to school, QM and KD decided that Miranda would take the dusted-with-gold invitations with her on her eighth day at Mountain River Valley Elementary.

When Miranda got to school early for her extra-extra Mandatory National Reading and Writing and Math Exam practice, Miss Kinde handed her a test and told her to get started while she went to make copies. Because the other students didn't need extra-extra practice, Miranda was alone.

Instead of starting her practice exam, Miranda took the invitations out of her bag, took a deep breath, and began putting them on desks. One invitation for Agatha and another for Agnes. She put an invitation on Donut's desk, then one on Norbert's, and another one on Norris's. She went to the next row and put one on Fletcher's desk and, pausing for a minute, one on Hillary Greenlight-Miller's. She kept going until she got to Maude's desk, which was empty except for a sticky spot in the middle, three pencils, and her You Journal. Miranda thought it still smelled like hard-boiled eggs.

She held her nose and lowered the invitation just as a breeze came through the open window. The breeze opened Maude's You Journal to the very first page, and the princess couldn't believe what she saw. Maude was drawing! Not writing! Drawing! Miranda saw the picture of a dreadful dog and a smiling Miss Kinde and the hard-boiled eggs.

And then she saw the pictures of her!

There was an enormous crown on top of her head! She'd never wear a crown to school. She didn't even like wearing them at royal events. They were heavy and made her head itch. Miranda turned the page and saw another drawing of her wearing shoes that looked like forks! Miranda turned the page and saw the worst drawing of all: She was holding her ruby pen and saying,

Miranda shut her eyes tightly and took a deep breath. Then she opened her eyes to make sure she was still alone. And then Princess Miranda shoved Maude's invitation back into her bag, sat down, and began her practice exam.

15

WHEN MISS KINDE CAME BACK IN

Miss Kinde noticed the invitations as soon as she walked back into 3B. Since rule number eighty-seven in the *Official Rules of Mountain River Valley Elementary* stated that invitations had to be given to everyone in the class, Miss Kinde scanned the room to make certain there was a gold envelope on every desk. She saw envelopes on Agatha's, Norbert's, Fletcher's, and Felix's desks. Hillary Greenlight-Miller had one, too. And Agnes and Donut and Desdemona. But just as Miss Kinde was about to check Maude's desk, Miranda sneezed seven times in a row.

Miss Kinde looked up. "Do you need a tissue?"

Miranda shook her head and pulled out a tissue from the diamond box in her bag. As she took it, her hand grazed the last birthday invitation. Miranda looked at Maude's desk and then at her teacher. But Miss Kinde was frantically stapling practice exams, so Miranda blew her nose and reread question three.

16

WHEN 3B CAME IN

When 3B trooped in, they were heartbroken to see another practice exam, but delighted to see the shiny gold envelopes on their desks. Moving the exams aside, 3B ripped open their invitations:

HER ROYAL MAJESTY
PRINCESS MIRANDA INVITES YOU
TO HER BIRTHDAY PARTY

SATURDAY, OCTOBER 1
NOON TO MIDNIGHT

HOT-AIR BALLOON RIDES, FASHION SHOW, CASTLE TOURS, TRAMPOLINES, OLYMPIC SOCCER, ELEPHANT RIDES, KARAOKE, SPA TREATMENTS, LIFE-SIZE PIÑATAS, ATV RIDES, BUILD YOUR OWN SUNDAE WITH NOT-YET-INVENTED ICE CREAM, MOVIES IN THE MOVIE THEATER, DONUTS, BOWLING, SWIMMING, MOON VIEWING WITH THE HUBBLE TELESCOPE, FIREWORKS, AND WHITE LION VIEWING.

A LEGAL GUARDIAN MUST SIGN THE WAIVER IN ORDER FOR YOU TO PARTICIPATE IN ANYTHING DANGEROUS.

As her classmates whispered and giggled and smiled big smiles at the princess, Maude, who had almost been late, moved her practice exam to the side to see if her envelope was under it. It wasn't. Maude looked under her desk, but nothing was on the floor. She scowled but didn't say anything. Instead, she opened her You Journal and began to write.

She's probably drawing another mean picture of me, the princess thought, *so it's only fair that I didn't invite her.*

17

WHAT MAUDE WROTE IN HER YOU JOURNAL

18

SUPER RARE IS SUPER COOL

3B couldn't stop chatting about the princess's party. No one in 3B had been to a party that lasted till the next day! In a castle!

"Is there really going to be a white lion?" Norbert asked the princess as 3B made their way to the cafeteria. "White lions are super rare."

"It's being flown in," the princess said, trying not to smell the day's lunch. "From . . . Belgrade." She was pretty sure that was what KD had said.

"Cool," Norbert said. "Super cool!"

It is cool, Miranda thought.

During lunch, Agatha and Agnes walked over to the princess.

"Will there really be a fashion show?" Agatha asked.

The princess nodded and tried not to look at their school lunches.

"With fancy clothes?" Agnes looked interested.

Miranda nodded again and tried not to notice Maude slowly nibbling her hard-boiled egg.

As soon as Agnes and Agatha went back to their seats, Donut slid over to the princess. "There'll be doughnuts? At your party?" he asked, then licked his lips.

Miranda didn't remember anything about doughnuts.

"It said doughnuts on the invitation," Donut said.

"Oh." The princess yawned. "There'll be doughnuts then. Plus cakes, cookies, pies, an ice cream bar, and candy." Miranda yawned again. School made her so very tired. And her head always ached.

"I just care about the doughnuts." Donut drooled onto the gloppy gray food on his tray. "I really love doughnuts."

"Okay," Miranda said, accidently looking at Maude, who was now reading a book called *Revenge Is a Dish Best Served Cold*.

At the end of the eighth day of school, like all the other days, Miranda was still exhausted, confused, and headachy. But one thing had changed. While the students in 3B were still staring at her, all of them (except one) were now smiling at her, too.

19

PICTURES ON THE WALL

After the dismissal bell rang on the eighth day of school, Maude walked home, ignored her happily clucking chickens, dragged herself up the twenty-seven stairs, and flung herself onto her bed, where she stared at the ceiling. A group of famous revolutionaries that she'd drawn stared back.

"Did any of you famous revolutionaries ever not get invited to a party?" she asked.

Because they were pictures of people who had died long ago, they didn't answer.

Maude turned onto her side and looked at a framed photograph of a woman holding a baby.

"I miss you, Mom," she said. "If you were alive, I might tell you how I didn't get an invitation to the stupid princess's party. Everyone else got one. Even my archenemy Hillary Greenlight-Miller." Maude touched the picture with her index finger. "I could file an official complaint with Principal Fish. The princess totally broke rule eighty-seven. But . . . I don't want to tell the principal." She picked up a stuffed ladybug. "If I tell Miss Kinde, she'll just feel sorry for me. That's not what I want."

What do you want? Maude imagined her mother asking.

She closed her eyes and imagined Principal Fish booming that rule 9,999 was that royalty would no longer be allowed at school. *No,* Maude thought. That would never be a rule. She opened her eyes.

Did you learn anything today? Maude imagined her dad asking.

Well, I learned that it feels awful to not get invited to something even if you don't want to go. I learned that all it takes for my classmates to be friends with someone rude is an invitation to pet a white lion. It isn't fair. The princess should learn something, too.

Yes, that's it! Maude thought with a jolt. *The princess should be taught a lesson!*

And who better to teach her than Maude?

20

A NOUN OR A VERB

That night Maude had a wonderful dream involving protest songs and spray paint, and when she woke up the next morning, she was eager to begin the ninth day of school.

"What's it called when a bunch of people decide not to do something?" she asked her dad and brother over breakfast.

"A boycott?" Walt asked, putting a spoonful of scrambled eggs on Maude's plate.

"Yes!" Maude grinned.

"Boycott can be a noun or a verb," Michael-John said.

"How do you boycott?" Maude asked.

"You have to get a large number of people to stop doing something all together," Michael-John explained.

Maude smiled. A boycott would be the perfect lesson to teach the pink princess. Miranda would definitely learn a lesson if no one went to her party! But how could Maude convince 3B not to go when that was all they talked about?

Maude spent hours jotting down notes in her You Journal. Here are the ideas she came up with:

<u>BIRTHDAY PARTY BOYCOTT IDEAS</u>

Tell 3B aliens have taken over the castle.
Tell 3B there's bubonic plague at the castle.
Pay 3B not to go to the party.

She also drew a lot of pictures:

21

HELP FROM MICHAEL-JOHN

When Maude got home from school on Friday, Walt was nowhere to be seen.

"Where's Dad?" she asked Michael-John, who was actually not in pajamas for once but was still hunched over his dictionaries.

"Beetle symposium. He'll be home for *cena*, which I just learned is Latin for dinner."

"Wasn't he just at a beetle conference?"

Michael-John nodded, but didn't look up. "There are a lot of beetles. And this is a symposium. Last week was a conference."

Maude sat in front of his stack of dictionaries. "I need your help. I'm having a boycott!"

"What are you boycotting?"

"Princess Miranda's birthday party."

"Why?"

"Well, she broke rule eighty-seven in the

Official Rules of Mountain River Valley Elementary." She petted Onion the Great Number Eleven. "Rule eighty-seven says if you give out invitations during school hours, you have to give one to everyone."

"And you didn't get one?"

Maude shook her head.

"Maybe you lost yours? You lose a lot of things."

"I might not be that organized, but even I can't lose something I never had." Maude took out her You Journal, which was strangely gummy. "The invitations were on *fourteen* desks. Not on mine. I looked. Everywhere."

"Oh."

"I'm tired of writing official letters of complaint to Principal Fish. He never answers. So, I'm going to have a boycott."

"You need numbers to boycott."

"I know! I'm going to get Three B to boycott, too. It's going to be my first official social justice movement!" She found her list in her You Journal and read him her three ideas.

"Those are all terrible ideas," her brother said. "First, no one will believe you about the aliens. If they do, it might make them want to go more. I'd *only* go to a princess party if there were aliens."

Maude nodded in sad agreement.

"And everyone knows that bubonic plague stopped being a real problem in 1959."

"Shucks," Maude said. "What about my last idea?"

"How much money do you have?"

Maude closed her eyes. "Nine dollars and seventeen cents."

Michael-John tapped his fingers on top of a dictionary. "That's about sixty-five cents per person."

Maude sighed.

"Oh well." Michael-John looked back at his dictionary.

Maude put on her glasses. "I need help! Please Michael-John! I need to boycott!"

"Why?"

"The princess is mean," Maude said. "She goes to school super early even though it's against school rules." She took her glasses off.

"You always say you want to get to school early. But then you oversleep and race around putting weird stuff in your pockets and end up late."

"It's not weird stuff," Maude said. "It's all the stuff I need for school."

"Maybe the princess goes to school early for extra help."

Maude ignored this possibility. "Well, it was her stupid ruby pen that got my hard-boiled eggs taken away and she never eats the school food or plays her recorder at music and she just stands there at PE and recess."

"Do you play the recorder?" Michael-John asked.

"Of course not! School recorders are gross.

And my harmonica sounds much better." Luckily Mr. Mancini, the music teacher, was around 182 years old and hadn't yet noticed her harmonica.

"You don't eat school food either," Michael-John said. "You bring your lunch."

"Not from a castle."

"You don't live in a castle."

"NO," Maude screeched. "I DON'T!"

"If you lived in a castle, you'd probably be a princess."

"I'm absolutely not a princess!"

Michael-John nodded calmly. "But if you were a princess, you'd bring your lunch from your castle."

Maude scowled. "I bring lunch from home, because Principal Fish still won't do anything about the Styrofoam lunch trays. You're not helping, Michael-John. How do I get Three B to join my boycott?"

"What about the truth?"

The truth, Maude thought. *The truth*? Should she tell 3B about the hard-boiled eggs and the bandana and how she was the only one in the whole class not to get invited?

It was so simple! Truth! Just five little letters. Could she do it? Could Maude Brandywine Mayhew Kaye, the roller-skating social justice revolutionary of Mountain River Valley Elementary, tell the truth?

22

MAUDE TELLS THE TRUTH

The next day was Saturday, which meant there was just one week before Princess Miranda's birthday party extravaganza. For the first time ever, Maude woke before her rooster crowed. She felt ready to tell the truth and organize a boycott!

She wore her JUSTICE FOR ALL sweatshirt, cargo pants, and VOTES FOR WOMEN sash. She tied the orange bandana around her head and put two pencils, her harmonica, a compass, three Band-Aids, and a small pack of ancient Rainbow Sweeties into her pockets. Then she stomped into the living room.

"I leave now, for Justice!" she told her dad, who was on his head, and her brother, who was reading the definition of the noun *fair shake*.

"*Fair shake* means fair chance or treatment," Michael-John said. "It was first used in 1930."

"Peace is its own reward," Walt said.

"I'm busy," Maude replied. "I don't have time for quotes or definitions, gentlemen."

"There's always time for quotes," Walt said. "Mahatma Gandhi once said, 'Peace is its own reward.' Do you know who he was?"

"He freed India from British rule," Maude said, putting two hard-boiled eggs into her last empty pocket.

"Yes. Mahatma Gandhi inspired movements for freedom around the world."

"I'm not sure when I'll be home."

"Be home by three, my lovely leaf beetle."

"I'll try," Maude said, strapping on her skates.

Using Mountain River Valley's official school directory, Maude found her classmates' addresses. She rang doorbells, buzzed buzzers, and knocked on doors with heavy brass knockers. And, when her classmates weren't home, Maude found them at soccer games, origami instruction, and indoor swimming pools. Maude's classmates thought it was strange that Maude had found them on a Saturday, but they also liked it. It made them feel special to have Maude skate over and say, "I must talk to you about something important!" With each classmate, Maude would take a deep breath and tell them how rude the princess had been about the hard-boiled egg and handkerchief.

Most of Maude's classmates thought it was super weird that Maude had offered the princess a hard-boiled egg. They also thought it was unusual that Maude had given the princess a handkerchief when there were boxes and boxes of tissues in 3B. And most of them just nodded as Maude talked about famous boycotts and social justice movements in history. But when she told them the real and painful truth, they all listened.

"The real and painful truth," Maude would say to Norbert or Agatha or whomever she was talking to, "is that Princess Miranda did not invite me to her birthday party."

Whomever Maude was talking to would look shocked.

"There was an invitation on everyone's desk. Except mine!"

"Really?" Fletcher or Felix or Desdemona would ask.

"Really! And even though I know it breaks rule eighty-seven, I'm not here about the rules. I'm here because the next time the princess has a party, she might not invite . . . you!"

Maude enjoyed watching the person across from her think about this. When it was clear they understood, she would take out her You Journal and have them sign under her Birthday Boycott Pledge with numbers one to fifteen. She had signed on the first line, and as she went from house to apartment building to soccer field, she filled up all the other lines, until there were just two more lines left to fill.

Unfortunately, the second-to-last person Maude needed to sign the Birthday Boycott Pledge was the annoying Hillary Greenlight-Miller, who was taking a practice Mandatory National Reading and Writing and Math Exam at the public library.

But five seconds into Maude's famous-boycotts-in-history speech, Hillary said, "I don't need a speech, Maude. I won't go to the party. You're right, Miranda *is* rude. I'm surprised I was invited."

Maude shoved a pencil into Hillary's hand.

When Hillary signed, Maude let out a sigh of relief. "Great," she said. "By the way, your answer to question seven is wrong."

After Hillary, Maude went to Donut's house. Donut listened as Maude described famous boycotts in history, as well as the story of the hard-boiled egg and the handkerchief. Of all the kids in 3B, Donut understood that Maude was trying to get her classmates to do something important. But Donut loved doughnuts so much that he couldn't imagine not eating them on purpose.

"I know it's hard, Donut," Maude said. "But we must stand together for Justice!"

Donut, imagining hundreds of doughnuts getting eaten by a white lion, frowned.

"We need to teach the princess a lesson. I was the only kid not invited to the party, remember?"

Donut nodded. He felt bad for Maude. Donut liked Maude, even though he also thought she was very unusual. He felt connected to her, because she knew what it felt like to have a parent who'd died. Donut's father had died, and even though he and Maude never talked about it, Donut felt comforted knowing that there was someone else who felt really sad some days.

His hand was trembling, but he took the pencil from Maude and signed: Duncan David Donatello.

Shocking them both, Maude hugged him.

Then, because she was so happy that she'd gotten every kid in 3B to sign the pledge, which meant she could have her first boycott and first official social justice movement, Maude shared her pack of Rainbow Sweeties with him.

Side by side, they sat on the front porch steps,

looking up at Mount Coffee and eating the stale candy. For a moment, Donut wished he'd gotten to know his dad long enough to find out what his favorite kind of doughnut was. For a moment, Maude wished she could have talked to her mom about having a princess in her class. And then, as their dead parents would have wanted, their minds turned to other things.

23

BIRTHDAY BOYCOTT PART ONE

The following Saturday, on the day of the royal birthday party, both Miranda and Maude woke up excited.

Maude whistled as she made her way down to the chicken coop. In just a few hours, Miranda's party would start, and what a shock it would be to that pink princess when no one came. She'd actually done it! The first of many social justice movements!

"Justice for all," Maude sang as she gathered the morning eggs.

"Bawk," Rosalie squawked.

"Good morning, my special Frizzle chicken!" Maude sang. But for some reason her voice sounded weak, not strong. "Your feathers look especially curly this morning."

"Bawk, bawk," Rosalie repeated, looking over

at the other chickens and General Cockatoo, the rooster, who were pecking together in the yard.

Maude looked at the other chickens and then back at Rosalie. "Are you feeling left out of the chicken games?" Maude asked.

Rosalie looked right at her. Could a chicken actually feel left out? *Was it possible that her fancy Frizzle chicken was sad?* Maude wondered. *Of course not*, she told herself, but for some reason she wasn't quite as happy walking up the twenty-seven stairs as she'd been walking down.

On the other side of town, KD and QM led Miranda to an enormous stack of birthday presents.

"Try to open your gifts quickly," KD said. "Since everyone will be coming soon."

Staring at the pile of presents, Miranda shuddered. *Not everyone*, she thought. She hadn't invited Maude. If QM and KD knew Miranda hadn't invited her, they'd probably be mad that she'd broken rule eighty-seven. Maude must have known she'd broken rule eighty-seven, because Maude seemed to know every rule ever invented. She also seemed to know how to finish practice exams quickly and how to avoid playing one of the gross recorders during music class. But still, it was good that Miranda hadn't invited her. Wasn't it?

"Aren't you going to open your present?" QM asked, giving Miranda a puzzled look.

Very slowly, the princess unwrapped the first of many presents before her.

Over at Maude's house, Walt cracked the morning eggs into a sizzling frying pan and said, "The Italian saint Thomas Aquinas once said, 'There is nothing on this earth more to be prized than true friendship.'"

"My chicken Rosalie doesn't seem to have any friends," Maude told him. "I don't know why. She's just like all the other chickens. I mean her feathers are curly since she's a Frizzle, but . . . she's still a chicken, right?"

Michael-John looked up from his dictionary. "A chicken is a chicken is a chicken."

Walt nodded in agreement. "The Irish writer Oscar Wilde once said, 'Be yourself; everyone else is already taken.' Perhaps your curly feathered Rosalie is just being herself."

"Yeah," Maude said. Of course, her chicken couldn't help but be herself. No one could be anything but themselves. Maude couldn't help but be herself. Hillary Greenlight-Miller probably couldn't help but be herself, either. No one could. Not even a princess.

"Eggs, my little stag beetle?" Walt asked.

"No," Maude said. "I'm not hungry."

Back in the castle, KD handed Miranda another gift.

Princess Miranda looked at it glumly.

"Shouldn't you be smiling rainbows?" KD asked. "It's your birthday!"

Miranda shrugged. "I don't feel like opening gifts," she said.

QM, shocked that her daughter didn't want more presents, put her hand on Miranda's forehead.

At the same moment, across town, Walt put his hand on his daughter's forehead, because Maude had never said no to eggs.

"Are you certain you don't want eggs?" Walt asked Maude.

"Go see the white lion," KD suggested. "He's terrifyingly beautiful."

"No, thanks," the princess and the not-a-princess said AT THE EXACT SAME TIME.

It had been a beautiful sunny day, but at that moment, a huge cloud passed over the sun, and everything went dark.

24

BIRTHDAY BOYCOTT PART TWO

Although Miranda's party began at noon, she stayed in her pajamas until 11:45 a.m. Then, because it was so late, she put on the first pink dress she saw, which didn't have a single ruffle or sequin. She stared at her shoe collection but decided to go barefoot.

At 11:58 a.m., Miranda walked down the grand staircase, where her parents were waiting. They were shocked by her shoeless feet but said nothing.

At 11:59 a.m., Miranda walked out to the great lawn, where the following happened:

- One dozen pink hot-air balloons rose into the air.
- Thirteen clowns poured out of a tiny automobile.

- The rare white lion roared a terrifying roar.
- Seven screeching monkeys wearing bowties cartwheeled in.
- The castle bells rang out twelve times.

Then everything went silent. Princess Miranda waited.

The clowns stopped laughing, the monkeys stopped screeching, the bells stopped ringing, and the white lion stopped roaring.

Miranda looked all around, and she knew. No one was coming.

25

BIRTHDAY BOYCOTT PART THREE

At the very moment Miranda realized no one was coming to her birthday party, Maude glumly put on a plain yellow T-shirt, brown overalls, and sneakers. Slowly, she tied her orange bandana around her neck and walked past Walt, who was standing on his head, and Michael-John, who was reading the definition of the word *onus* (which is a noun meaning burden or blame).

When Maude opened the door, Rudolph Valentino rushed past her and down into the yard. Sluggishly, Maude clomped down the twenty-seven steps after him and knelt beside her huge but tomato-less tomato plant. "Not one tomato? Not one?" Suddenly furious, she began ripping it out of the ground.

When General Cockatoo suddenly crowed, Maude stopped tearing up her plant. She looked

at the dirt in her hands and then over at her rooster, who was hanging with a group of chickens under a shady tree. Then Maude looked at Rosalie in the chicken coop all alone. She imagined Miranda all alone at her party.

Maude wiped the dirt off her hands and rubbed her eyes. Picturing a girl all alone at a party made Maude feel terrible. She knew what that was like. She'd been to parties where everyone else was so busy playing together that they never noticed her swinging alone.

And now Maude had caused that to happen! Her boycott was making someone feel awful! It wasn't social justice at all! Maude pulled her bandana over her eyes, which were tearing. *Ugh,* she thought. Her bandana smelled terrible! She really needed to wash it. No wonder Miranda hadn't wanted to use it on her sneezy nose.

"What have I done?" Maude asked Rudolph Valentino, her stinky bandana, and the broken tomato plant.

Of course, neither the dog nor the bandana nor the plant could answer.

26

BIRTHDAY BOYCOTT PART FOUR

At 12:05 p.m., Princess Miranda sat down at a party table and put her head on her arms.

At 12:06 p.m., Maude put Rudolph Valentino's leash on and yelled that she was going to take a walk.

"Be home by three!" Walt called.

"I'll try!" Maude yelled back.

"Don't forget what the Greek storyteller Aesop said," Walt called down. "'No act of kindness, no matter how small, is ever wasted.'"

27

WHO DOESN'T LOVE CHICKENS?

Without looking at her compass, Maude took eleven lefts and three rights away from her house and, to her surprise, ended up at the very back edge of the castle. She thought about turning around, but instead, she took a step closer. From where she was, she could see ten million pink balloons, a chocolate statue of Miranda, and many adorable monkeys. She took another step and could see the table of doughnuts, a tiny automobile, and a slumped pink figure with bare feet. Maude put on her glasses, took a last step, and stuck her head into an opening in the gate.

At that moment, Miranda looked up and saw Maude. The princess might have been confused by everything in school, but when she saw Maude, she was 100 percent certain that Maude had ruined her party.

When Maude saw Miranda looking at her, she knew that the princess knew that she, Maude, had ruined the party.

Miranda glared at Maude. She hadn't been invited! Why was she here?

But why hadn't Miranda invited her? Because of a dumb drawing in a dumb notebook? *It must have felt awful to be the only one without the gold envelope on her desk*, Miranda thought.

Miranda must feel terrible to have no one here, Maude thought. School must be kind of terrible for her, too, since the kids in 3B always stared at her instead of asking her to play on the monkey bars or run around screaming. Maude tried to imagine Miranda running around the playground screaming, but she couldn't. This made Maude a tiny bit happy because she much preferred swinging quietly high above the screaming. Maude wondered what the princess thought about swings.

The two girls looked at one

another for a very long time.

And then Maude yelled, "ARE THOSE RAINBOW SWEETIES?"

Are those Rainbow Sweeties? was probably not the best way to end the silent staring. But Maude loved Rainbow Sweeties just as much as Donut loved doughnuts and Miranda loved rearranging all her fancy pink princess things.

Miranda was quiet for so long that Maude thought she hadn't heard her. But then the princess yelled, "YES, THOSE ARE RAINBOW SWEETIES."

At that moment, the white lion roared so ferociously that both girls jumped out of their skin and looked at each other. Then they looked at the white lion, who looked very hungry.

Then something amazing happened. Miranda stood up, went over to the Rainbow Sweeties, scooped some into a bowl, and walked over to Maude.

"Here." Miranda pushed the bowl into Maude's hand. Her *here* was Miranda's way of saying she was sorry that she hadn't invited Maude to the party.

Shocked, Maude pulled her head out of the gate. "Really?"

Miranda nodded.

Maude took the bowl and gulped a handful of candy. Then she remembered the quote Walt had told her about kindness. "Do you want some?" she asked. Maude's *do you want some* was her way of saying she was sorry her boycott had been so successful. And that she'd brought in so many hard-boiled eggs. If she was being honest, she would have admitted that having so many on her desk had been annoying. Maude didn't know that the princess had seen the drawings in her You Journal, but if she did, she would have been sorry about that, too.

Miranda shook her head. "I don't like candy."

Maude was shocked. "Really? What about cake?"

The princess shook her head. "But there's

a very big one if you want some." She pointed toward an enormous pink cake in the middle of the great lawn.

"What about ice cream? Everyone likes ice cream."

"Not me," Miranda said quietly. "I find it too cold. And too sweet."

Maude couldn't believe her ears! Too sweet? "What about doughnuts?" she asked. "Cupcakes? Pudding? Cookies? Pie?" Maude's eyes grew wider as she gobbled another handful of Rainbow Sweeties.

The princess shook her head. "I don't have a sweet tooth."

Maude thought it was incredible that someone her age didn't like dessert.

Miranda sighed.

"Don't feel bad," Maude said quickly. "Sugar is terrible. I have nine cavities. That's a lot for someone my age. My dad isn't strict about anything except for sugar. He hates it! You're more likely to find an antique butterfly sword in my house than one cube of sugar!"

"I don't have any cavities," Miranda said, wondering what an antique butterfly sword was.

"Your teeth are very sparkly and clean."

Miranda nodded, but not rudely.

The girls stared at each other, and then Miranda said, "Wow! You ate that candy fast! Do you want more?" She sounded impressed.

When Maude nodded, the princess pushed a button, the gates opened, and Maude Brandywine Mayhew Kaye entered the castle grounds to follow Princess Miranda across the great lawn.

Then the white lion roared again, which scared the girls so much that their knees and elbows bumped against one another.

"Do you want to get out of here?" Maude asked the princess. "That lion is terrifying. And my dog is really scared." She pointed to Rudolph Valentino, who was shaking and peeing in a far corner of the lawn next to a giant bronze statue of the royal family.

"That's a dog?" Miranda squinted. "I thought it was a rat. A giant rat or a very ugly cat. I hate dogs. I'm terrified of dogs."

Maude smiled kindly at the princess. "Rudolph Valentino is the world's most amazing dog. That's a fact. You're going to love him."

With those five little words, something amazing happened in Miranda's brain. She heard "You're going to love him" as *You're going to love my dog because we're going to be friends and everything is going to get much better.*

"Where do you want to go?" Miranda asked nervously. "Blake, my chauffeur, can only drive me within the town limits."

Maude laughed. "We don't need a ride! We're not climbing Mount Coffee! We'll walk to my house, which is really close. If we go the back way, we're practically neighbors. You can meet my chickens!"

Walk? Miranda thought. *You want me to walk somewhere?* She looked down at her feet. It was so weird that she wasn't wearing shoes. "Chickens?" she squeaked out instead.

"Yes! Who doesn't love chickens? I sing to my chickens, so they are the funniest, happiest, most beautiful birds in all the land!"

Miranda continued to stare at her shoeless feet. *Could* she *love chickens?* The princess looked up from her feet and out at the balloons, monkeys, and white lion.

"Plus," Maude said, dumping more Rainbow Sweeties into her pockets and putting her glasses back on, "unlike that terrifying white lion, my chickens won't bite."

The princess looked at Maude, took a deep breath, and said, "Okay. Let's walk to your house."

28

ALL OF THE AMAZING THINGS THAT HAPPENED NEXT

1. Maude went inside the castle while she waited for Miranda to get permission to come over.
2. Miranda asked KD and QM if she could walk to a classmate's house to see some chickens. One of which had curly feathers.
3. "Go," QM said. "Have a wonderful time!"
4. "Don't you want shoes?" KD asked.
5. Miranda ran up to her room, opened her closet, and put on shoes that were almost comfortable!
6. Miranda walked one point two miles! On her own feet!
7. While walking, Miranda thought about calling Blake for a ride 127 times, but she didn't.
8. On a good day, Maude's chickens are

beautiful and hilarious. On this Saturday, they were truly amazing and spectacular.

9. In thirty minutes, both girls were laughing.
10. Most of the girls' laughter was because of the chickens.
11. Some of Maude's laughter was because of all the Rainbow Sweeties she'd eaten.
12. Some of Miranda's laughter was because she'd thrown the world's worst party, was outside the castle by herself, was making a friend, and had walked one point two miles! On her own two feet!
13. Rosalie laid an egg right in front of Miranda.
14. "Weird," Maude said to the princess. "That's her second egg today. It must be a lucky egg. Do you want to get it? Collecting chicken eggs is fun."
15. The princess thought about saying

no way, but instead she walked toward Rosalie and picked up the egg, which was still warm.

16. "Be careful," Maude said. "It's very delicate."
17. "That I know," the princess replied, extremely relieved that just-laid chicken eggs didn't smell nearly as bad as hard-boiled ones.
18. Maude and Miranda carried Rosalie's egg into the house, which meant that Miranda walked up twenty-seven crooked stairs on her own two feet.
19. Michael-John, who was reading dictionaries in his bathrobe, barely looked up when he heard that there was a princess in his house.
20. Walt was not standing on his head.
21. Miranda met Walt, Michael-John, and Onion the Great Number Eleven.
22. Walt, Michael-John, and Onion the Great Number Eleven met Miranda.
23. Walt took Rosalie's egg and some other eggs and made a delicious omelet for

Maude and Miranda, who realized they were both starving.

24. Miranda was making a friend.
25. Maude was making a friend.
26. In just six hours, the princess and the absolutely not a princess discovered that they had lots to talk about, including: the wonderfulness of Miss Kinde, the awfulness of Hillary Greenlight-Miller, the loudness

of Principal Fish, the grossness of school lunches, the yuckiness of the practice Mandatory National Reading and Writing and Math Exam, and the greatness of cheese.

27. It turned out that Maude and Miranda both really loved cheese!
28. When it was time for Miranda to go home, she was shocked to see it was nearly dark. She'd never spent so long laughing with someone her age.
29. Walt gave the girls headlamps, and they walked the one point two miles back, which meant that in one day, Miranda had walked two point four miles! On her very own feet!
30. Maude would have walked back to her house, but because it was dark, QM and KD insisted that Blake drive her, so Maude got to ride in the fancy automobile!

29

FANTASTIC THINGS AND INCREDIBLE IDEAS

After all the amazing things that happened after the birthday boycott, the princess and the absolutely not a princess were friends. Friends! Maude Brandywine Mayhew Kaye and Princess Miranda Rose Lapointsetta talked and whispered and giggled with each other so much that Miss Kinde often thought about separating them. She didn't, though. Partly because she liked alphabetical order, but mostly because she was so pleased to see two girls who had seemed so different discover they had so much in common.

With the exception of Hillary Greenlight-Miller, 3B was happy that Maude and the princess were friends. Hillary was jealous that she didn't have a princess for a best friend, and she devoted even more time to her Saturday practice Mandatory National Reading and Writing

and Math Exams. For about a week, Donut was irritated that the table of birthday doughnuts had been devoured by the insatiable white lion instead of him, but eventually he got over it.

Amazing things started happening for Miranda now that she had a friend. Because she walked over to Maude's house a lot, she was finally getting enough exercise and went right to sleep on school nights, which meant she wasn't so tired at school. Not being so tired meant she understood more, too. She still needed extra-extra help, but Maude was almost as good at explaining things as Miss Kinde.

Maude discovered that it was fun to help a best friend learn new things. And some days Maude learned from Miranda! She didn't learn new vocabulary words or how to grow tomatoes, but she learned that if she laid out her clothes the night before like the princess did, then she could almost make it to school on time. Maude also learned that hanging out with a friend in a castle was even better than she could have imagined.

Castles, it turned out, were not only full of rare books, uncomfortable furniture, and very large paintings. They were also full of candy, water-beds, and really big televisions! Even though Maude was into justice for all, growing tomatoes, and taking long walks, she also really loved tele-vision. Walt felt the same way about television as he did about sugar, so Maude didn't have a tele-vision at her house.

One recent Saturday morning, Maude roller-skated over to the castle with Rudolph Valentino.

"Hello!" she called to QM and KD, who, as usual, were sitting on their uncomfortable couch in their uncomfortable clothes in one of the castle's beautiful sitting rooms.

"Good morn—" QM and KD called as Maude flew past them and up to Miranda's wing.

"I'm starving!" Maude announced to the princess, who was organizing her nail polishes. "I'm just going to call the kitchen and order a little something." She pushed the castle intercom button down to the kitchen.

The princess smiled to herself, since Maude had said the same exact thing last Saturday and the Saturday before that.

By the time Chef Blue knocked on the princess's door to deliver Maude's banana split with extra hot fudge on the side, bowl of Rainbow Sweeties, and French fries, Maude was completely zoned out in front of the enormous television. Miranda put down the bottle of "plumtastic plum" and walked across the room to get Maude's food.

"Thank you," Miranda said to Chef Blue.

"You're most welcome," Chef Blue replied, grinning at Maude, who was grinning at the TV. Even if it was much too early for dessert, Chef Blue loved being able to finally make sweets for a child.

Miranda brought Maude her food and went back to her polishes. But after she finished putting "lovely lemon" next to "midnight madness" she decided she was bored.

"Let's do something," Miranda said.

Maude nodded at the TV.

"Maude," Miranda said a little louder.

"How adorable," Maude cooed to the pair of juggling cats.

Miranda walked in front of the TV and started doing jumping jacks.

"You're blocking the enormous television," Maude whined.

"Let's *do* something," Miranda said. "I don't want to watch TV all day."

"You don't?" Maude asked.

"No." Miranda said. "Let's go to your house. Did you collect eggs? I miss the chickens."

"The chickens are molting," Maude said.

"Molting means losing or shedding feathers," the princess replied.

"Good practice Mandatory National Reading and Writing and Math Exam word!" Maude looked away from the TV and smiled at her friend. "But when chickens molt they stop laying eggs." She dipped a French fry in hot fudge and looked back at the TV. "Let's hang out here till lunch."

The princess felt disappointed. Lunch wasn't for several hours, and now that she went to school, she'd gotten used to spending time out of the castle. The things at Maude's house weren't fancy, but they were always fascinating. Not only was there Walt's enormous beetle collection, there were also things like pirate swords and false-teeth bottle openers just lying around. At the castle, most of the really interesting things were locked away.

"I want to do something now," Miranda said.

"Like what?"

Miranda looked around. She noted the neatly arranged fashion magazines on her desk, the fabric samples near her closet, and Rudolph Valentino curled up on her bed. She walked over and gave him a pet, then looked at Maude, who was wearing orange overalls and a brand-new, almost-clean purple bandana. Maude had kicked off her shoes and roller skates. Her socks, Miranda noticed, were an odd shade of green and full of holes. Then Miranda looked at her almost perfectly alphabetized nail-polish collection.

"I have an idea!" She smiled.

"What?" Maude asked, suddenly nervous.

"Let's paint your toenails."

Maude put on her glasses and stared at Miranda.

"I'll take it off if you don't like it," Miranda said. "Promise."

"I won't like it," Maude said. She pushed her glasses up to the top of her head. "I refuse pink."

Miranda scanned her polishes until she landed on "transcendent turquoise." She held it up. "How's this?"

Maude sighed. "Don't tell anyone. Whoever heard of a social justice activist with fancy feet?"

"I won't."

"And," Maude said, "if I let you polish my toes, you're going to have to do something, too."

"Like what?"

"I'll think of something." Maude smiled mischievously. "But don't worry, I won't make you eat a hard-boiled egg." Now that Maude knew how much Miranda hated hard-boiled eggs, she only ate them when the princess wasn't around.

Miranda began painting her best friend's toes. A long time passed, and then she stepped away. "It's amazing," the princess said. Maude's feet did look incredible.

"I can't look," Maude said, covering her eyes.

"Really?" Miranda was disappointed, but not surprised.

"Sorry," Maude said. "I'm ready to walk back to my house now so you can have your turn." She swallowed the last French fry and tried to give Miranda her most sinister smile.

Truthfully, Maude was having a hard time deciding what she could have Miranda do in exchange for the nail polish on her toes. She tried to come up with a brilliant idea while the two girls walked back to her house, checked on the still-molting chickens, and climbed up the slightly crooked twenty-seven stairs into her house. Unfortunately, the princess had already organized all Maude's overdue library books (by color) and straightened all of the protest posters on her walls. She could have Miranda rearrange her closet, which was about to explode, but that would be too much fun for the princess. Maude looked around her room, hoping for an idea as bananas as nail polish.

Her eyes landed on the big pile of dirty clothes on her floor. *Eureka*, she thought, scooping up an armful and walking over to her friend, who was singing to Rudolph Valentino.

"Here ya go," Maude said, holding out a bright orange T-shirt and a pair of cargo pants with holes in the knees.

The princess looked up from the dog. "These are your clothes," she said.

Maude grinned.

"What . . . do you want me to do with them?"

Organize them, the princess hoped Maude would say. She'd like nothing more than to tidy Maude's very messy room.

"Wear them." Maude smiled. "It's your part of the deal." She waved her foot in front of the princess. The shiny blue polish gleamed in the sunlight streaming through Maude's window.

Maude's toenails did look terrific, but the princess felt ill. Even though having a best friend had made her much happier, she was still picky about clothes. But she knew that a deal was a deal, so she slowly took off her fancy shoes, silk pants, and very expensive shirt. Reminding herself how much better school was with a friend, she slid into Maude's filthy pants. Next, she put on the stained orange shirt that read I'M + I LOST AN ELECTRON, a joke that she didn't get because she was still behind in science.

When she looked in Maude's mirror, Miranda did a double take. Everything was small, smelled like chicken feathers, and felt strangely warm. On the other hand, nothing poked or itched. Maude's dirty clothes felt soft and broken in.

Miranda hadn't felt this comfortable ever.

Maude picked up one of Miranda's golden shoes. "This is really heavy," she said. "How do you wear it?"

"On my foot," the princess said.

Maude put the shoe on. Then she put on the other one and attempted to stand up.

Miranda tried to hide her giggle as she looked at Maude wearing the gold shoes.

Maude looked at Miranda in the I'M + I LOST AN

ELECTRON shirt and turned her laugh into a cough.

Michael-John knocked on the door. "Dad wants to know if the princess and the absolutely not a princess want vittles," he said. "*Vittles* is a plural noun that means food. Right now, it's lunch."

"What's for lunch?" Miranda asked through the closed door.

"Stinky bishop cheese, bread, and tomatoes—not from Maude's garden," Michael-John replied.

Stinky bishop cheese, the princess thought, rubbing Maude's shirt. That sounded like it would smell. Not that long ago, she never would've let anyone see her in Maude's clothes. But having had twenty-seven days of best friendship, she knew that if life were to be an amazing adventure, you had to try a new cheese every now and then.

"Don't laugh," Maude told her brother as she opened the door.

As soon as Michael-John saw Maude and Miranda, he howled with laughter. When he finally stopped laughing, he took Maude's glasses from the top of her head and handed them to the princess.

"Do I have to?" Miranda asked.

"Yes," Michael-John said. "Maude isn't Maude without her glasses."

Miranda sighed and put the glasses on.

And then, in a flash, the world to Princess Miranda was CLEAR!

For the first time, the princess noticed the scar on Michael-John's chin, the blueness of Maude's eyes, how lovely Rudolph Valentino's fur really was.

"Miranda?" Maude and Michael-John asked together, staring at the princess.

But Miranda couldn't speak. Her eyes grew wide as she walked around the house, noticing the masks on the walls, the plants in the living room, the containers of preserved beetles, and the pile of dictionaries on the dining room table. In a daze, she couldn't stop marveling at the clear and colorful world she lived in.

"Miranda?" Maude asked her friend with great concern. "Are you okay?"

Miranda looked up to Maude and Michael-John's curious faces. "I can see!" she exclaimed. "And my headache is gone!"

30

WHERE THE STORY ENDS

Sadly, this is the end. Except in many ways, just like the friendship between absolutely not a princess Maude Brandywine Mayhew Kaye and Princess Miranda Rose Lapointsetta, it's just the beginning. There's much more ahead!

On this lovely autumn afternoon, the two friends are laughing as they walk on their own two feet. There they go, arm in arm, one in fancy shoes, the other smelling like chickens, headed in the direction of clear sight, school, friendship, and even more amazing adventures.

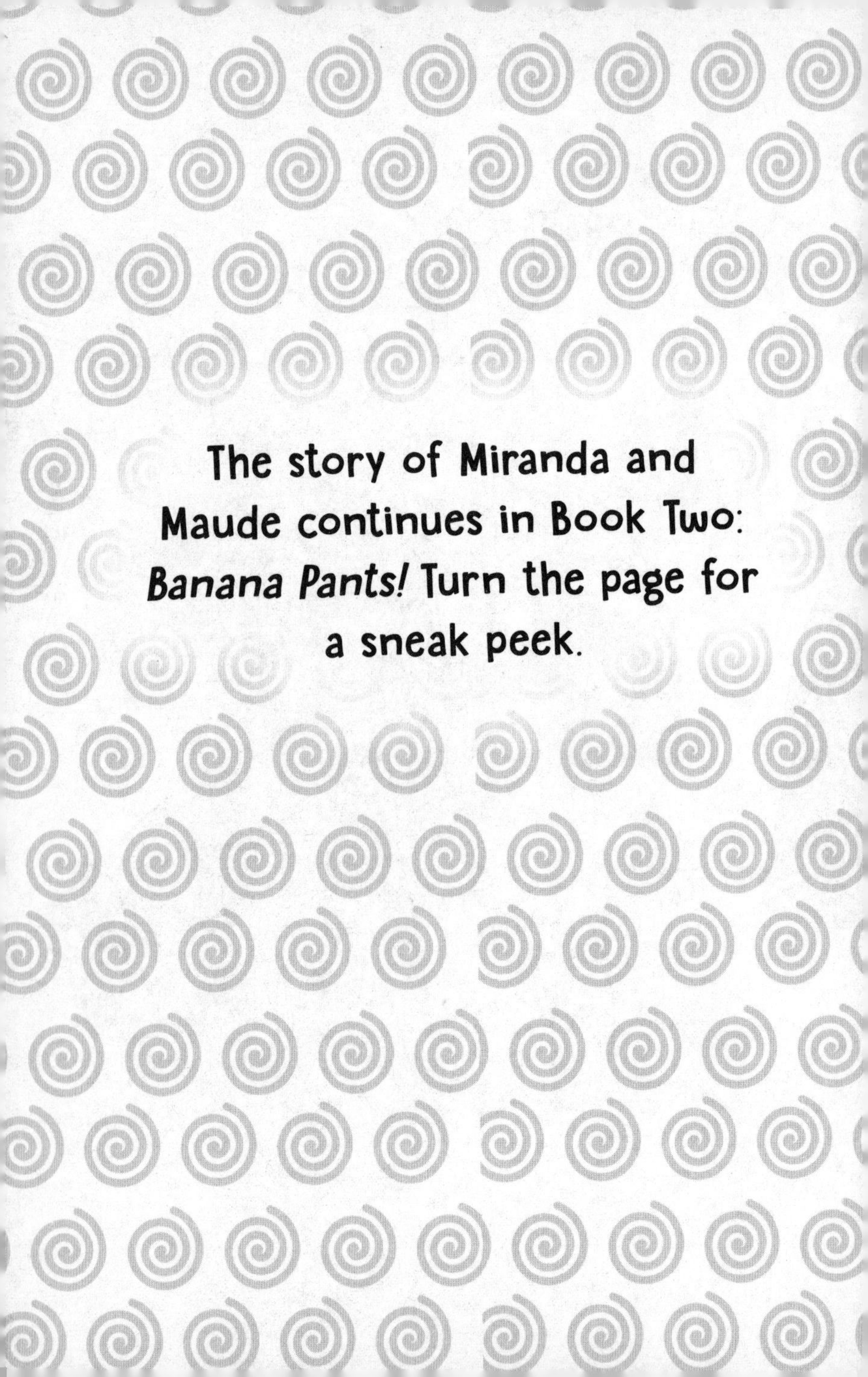

The story of Miranda and Maude continues in Book Two: *Banana Pants!* Turn the page for a sneak peek.

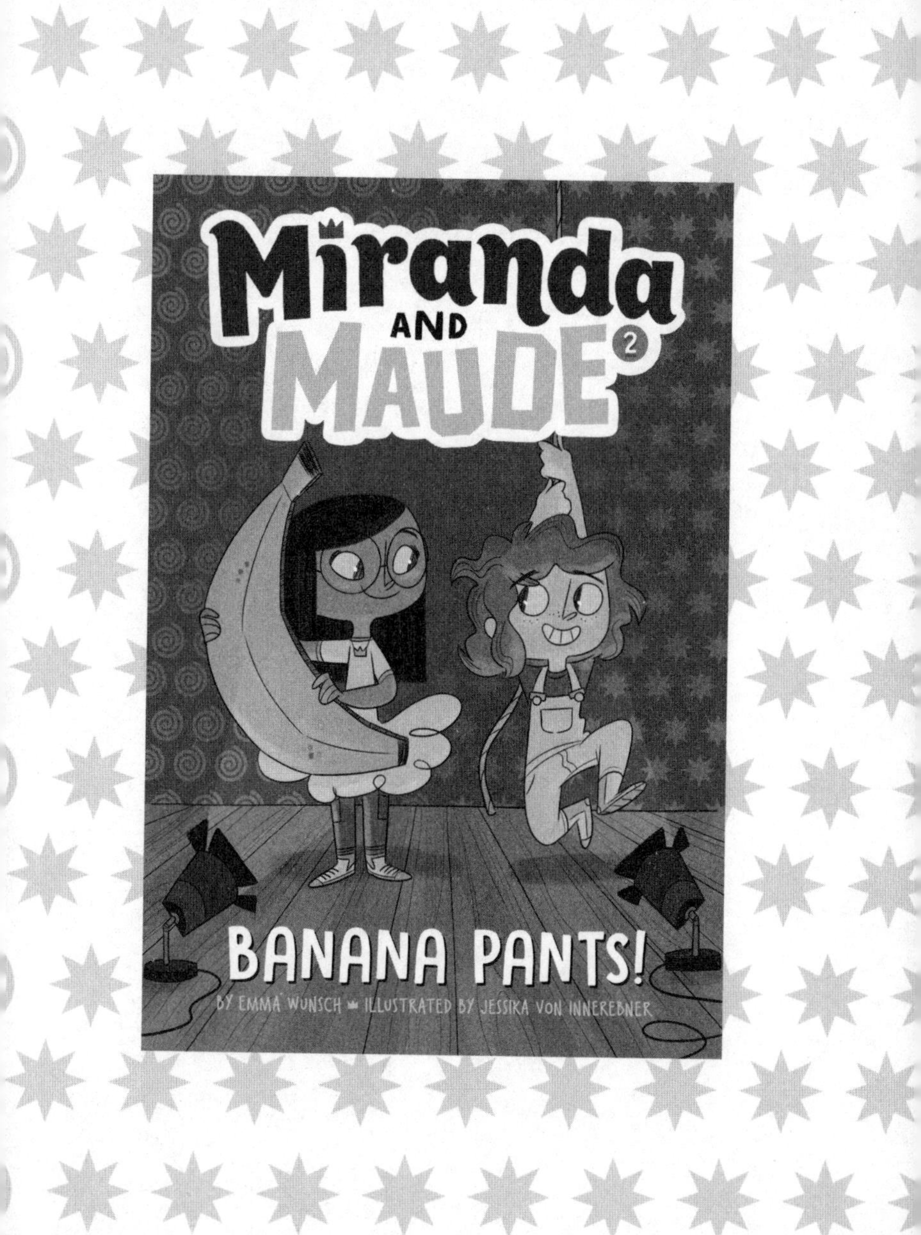
Miranda
AND
MAUDE
2
BANANA PANTS!
BY EMMA WUNSCH
ILLUSTRATED BY JESSIKA VON INNEREBNER

1

EXTRA-EXTRA EARLY MONDAY MORNING

One Monday morning, Princess Miranda Rose Lapointsetta went into her classroom, 3B, at Mountain River Valley Elementary extra-extra early. She was there for extra-extra help from her favorite teacher, Miss Kinde.

Before this year, Miranda had never been to school. She was a princess who lived in a castle and had a very old tutor who didn't teach her much. When Madame Cornelia retired, Miranda's parents (Queen Mom and King Dad, or QM and KD for short) made her go to school. At first, school was terrible. It smelled like hard-boiled eggs, everything was loud and confusing, and she always had a headache. Worst of all, she had no friends.

But then a bunch of things happened, and Miranda became best friends with Maude

Brandywine Mayhew Kaye, who was absolutely not a princess. Once Miranda had a friend and learned she needed glasses, she began to enjoy school. Things she once hated, like music class (which was very loud), lunch (which was very smelly), and PE (which was a little bit dangerous) were now practically okay, because everything was better when you had a friend to agree with you about how loud, smelly, and dangerous things were.

But right now, Miranda's classroom was not loud or smelly or dangerous. 3B was quiet, because she was the only student there, and it smelled like lavender, because that was what Miranda's beloved teacher, Miss Kinde, smelled like. Miss Kinde was just like her name. Kind! Wonderful! Amazing! She was always interested in what Miranda had to say and, best of all, even though she often reminded Miranda and Maude to stop talking to each other, she never switched their seats!

The only bad thing about Miss Kinde's class, Miranda thought that early Monday morning, *isn't about Miss Kinde at all*. It was about a test.

A famously awful test called the Mandatory National Reading and Writing and Math Exam, which every student had to take at the end of the school year. Since the beginning of the year (which wasn't that long ago), Miss Kinde had given 3B many, many practice exams. Because Miranda had never taken the exam before, and since Principal Fish thought it was extremely

important, she often had to spend her extra-extra help time taking a practice test.

"I'm sorry to give you another exam," Miss Kinde said sadly, handing Miranda a thick booklet.

"It's not your fault," Miranda said unhappily. Not only were the practice exams long, they were also confusing and boring. The exams caused fear and misery in both students and teachers alike. They took up time from the things the students and teachers really wanted to do.

Sighing, Miranda looked at the clock, grabbed a pencil from Maude's desk, and waited for Miss Kinde to tell her to begin.

But before Miss Kinde could say "begin," Maude Brandywine Mayhew Kaye roller-skated into the classroom yelling, "HELP!"

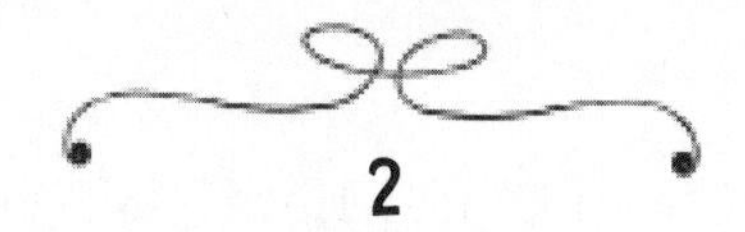

2

MAUDE BRANDYWINE MAYHEW KAYE TRULY NEEDS HELP

Miss Kinde and Miranda stood up. Did Maude need help stopping? But Maude came to an easy stop, plunked down on Miranda's desk, and took off her skates.

"What are you doing here?" Miranda asked. She was shocked to see her best friend, who often slept through her alarm clock (a crowing rooster named General Cockatoo) and always arrived almost-late to school.

"I saw the sunrise over Mount Coffee!" Maude said excitedly.

"That's wonderful," Miss Kinde said. "And it's wonderful to see you, Maude, but you do remember rules forty-six and fifty-eight?"

Rule forty-six in the *Official Rules of Mountain River Valley Elementary* said that students were not allowed in school until 7:42 a.m. unless they were getting help. Rule fifty-eight said that wheeled shoes were forbidden in school.

"I know *all* the rules," Maude said. "And I truly need help!"

Miss Kinde smiled at Maude, who was wearing paint-splattered pants, a wrinkled T-shirt that said SAVE THE HUMPHEAD WRASSE, and a pair of glasses that she loved but didn't need.

"I don't think you need help," Miss Kinde said

patiently. "You did tremendously well on Friday's practice exam."

"Did I beat Hillary?" Maude asked. She moved her glasses onto the top of her head.

Hillary was Hillary Greenlight-Miller, Maude's archenemy and the only person in 3B who did not dread practice exams.

Miss Kinde did not answer Maude's question.

"Never mind," Maude said. "It's not important! What's important are these!" She took a stack of letters out of her messenger bag. "Everyone keeps saying no!" Maude cried. "I write letter after letter demanding change and nothing ever happens."

"What kind of change?" Miss Kinde asked gently.

"Change for good!" Maude held out a letter. "Except no one will change! I wrote to Chemical Apple to say that they should stop putting chemicals on their apples. Do you know what they wrote back?"

Miss Kinde and Miranda shook their heads. Maude read:

Dear Maude Brandywine Mayhew Kaye,

Thank you for yet another letter suggesting Chemical Apple Inc. stop using chemicals on our apple trees. Unfortunately, at this time, that is impossible.

Sincerely,

E. Vole Mann McGoo
President, Chemical Apple Inc.

"Oh dear." Miss Kinde cleared her throat and looked at the clock. They were dangerously close to running out of time for Miranda's exam.

"*Impossible?!*" Maude bellowed. "It's *not* impossible! When you do something wrong, you apologize. You say, 'Sorry, that was a terrible idea. I won't do it ever again'!"

Miss Kinde nodded, but Miranda yawned. She couldn't help it. Maude was her absolutely positively best friend, but not everything that interested Maude interested her. Some things, like whatever Maude was talking about right now, really bored her.

Maude had her hand in a fist and was talking quickly to Miss Kinde. "I did exactly what you told me, Miss Kinde. I said what the problem was and explained why it's bad. But every letter I get back says the same thing! 'We're going to keep fishing,' 'We're going to keep poisoning apples,' 'We can't clean the lake,' 'Styrofoam forever'!"

"Styrofoam?" Miss Kinde asked.

"Principal Fish," Maude groaned. "No matter

how many times I tell him that Styrofoam is terrible, he won't do anything about the lunch trays."

Miss Kinde coughed a little. "Maude, it's inspiring to see how much you care about world issues. I am impressed with your many good causes, and I know how disappointed you must be."

"I am *terribly* disappointed. What should I do, Miss Kinde? I need help," Maude begged.

Miss Kinde hesitated and then said, "Well, maybe some of your classmates could write letters, too. Sometimes it helps if there's more than

one voice." She glanced at Miranda, who seemed to be falling asleep.

Maude looked at Miranda. "I could write so many more letters if you wrote letters, too!"

Miranda yawned again and shook her head. There was no way she was writing letters! "I'm really busy," she told Maude, pointing to the practice exam on her desk.

"Too busy to save the world?" Maude asked. "Too busy for peace and justice and a clean earth?"

But you're not actually saving the world, Miranda thought, looking at the pile of Maude's letters. *You're probably just giving yourself a hand cramp and wasting ink.*

"What do you care about?" Maude asked Miranda. "You must care about something."

"I care about lots of things," Miranda said quietly. "But letter writing is not one of them."

The girls looked at each other. Even though they were extremely different, they always got along. And now it wasn't that they were fighting exactly. But no matter how much Maude wanted her to, Miranda just couldn't care about letter writing.

No one said anything. Miss Kinde sneezed, and Miranda and Maude both handed her a tissue. Miss Kinde blew her nose and looked at the clock.

And then Walter Matthews Mayhew Kaye the eighth walked into 3B.

ACKNOWLEDGMENTS

This book is for my daughters, Georgia and Dahlia. Without the two of you, the two girls in this book wouldn't exist.

EMMA WUNSCH

Emma Wunsch is the author of *The Movie Version*, a young adult novel. This is her first chapter book. She lives in Lebanon, New Hampshire, with her husband and two daughters.

VISIT HER ONLINE AT
EMMAWUNSCH.COM
AND MIRANDAANDMAUDE.COM

JESSIKA VON INNEREBNER

Jessika von Innerebner is an artist who's worked with clients including Disney, Nickelodeon, Highlights, and Fisher-Price. She lives in Kelowna, Canada.

VISIT HER ONLINE AT JESSVONI.COM

READ THESE OTHER GREAT CHAPTER BOOKS!

OPTiCAL iLLUSiON FLiP BooK

ASTOUNDING OPTICAL ILLUSIONS

Gyles Brandreth

SCHOLASTIC INC.

New York Toronto London Auckland Sydney
Mexico City New Delhi Hong Kong Buenos Aires

Contents

Introduction

When is a short line really a long line? When is a number really a letter?

When it's an optical illusion!

Boggle your brain and dazzle your eyes with this tricky collection of great illusions. What you think you see is very different from what's actually on the page. And just when you're truly convinced that you can't believe your eyes anymore, flip the book and find another book in the back! There you'll discover even more deceptive puzzles, plus all kinds of optical tricks and experiments where you can create your very own illusions.

When is one book really two books? When it's the Optical Illusion Flip Book!

Is Seeing Believing?

To begin with, take a close look at this shape:

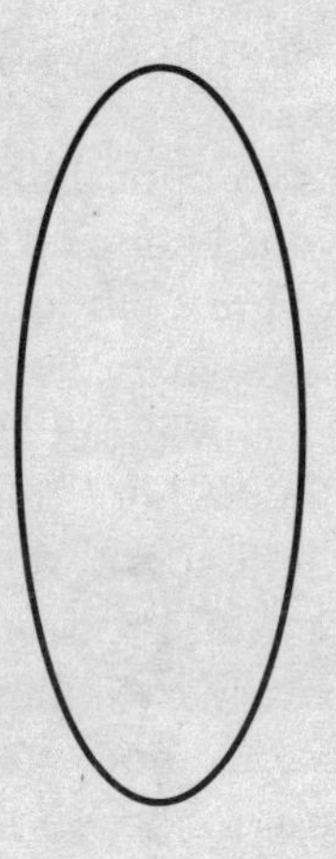

Do you agree that no one could possibly describe that shape as a perfect circle? Good. Now look at the picture of the bicycle on the next page. How would you describe the shape of the bicycle's front wheel? As a circle? Of course, because you *know* that a bicycle wheel has a circular shape.

The artist drew exactly the same shape above—that obviously isn't a circle—as he did to make the bicycle wheel—that obviously is a circle! But while you are looking at the same shape on both this page and the next, you realize that the bicycle wheel has to be circular even when it doesn't *seem* to be.

How to do the trick

Fill a glass about ⅔ full of water and drop a coin into the glass. Next, place a saucer over the glass and carefully turn the glass over. Invite your friends to look down into the glass. Incredibly, they will see not one coin, but two—one resting on the saucer at the "bottom" of the glass, and one floating on top of the water!

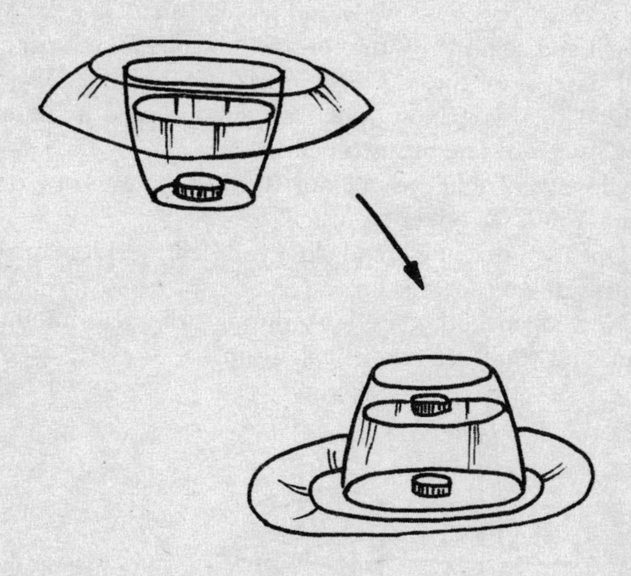

How the trick works

The reason you see two coins when only one coin really exists also has to do with the way light bends when it travels through different substances.

When the light rays reflected by the coin leave the water, they bend slightly before they enter your eye. However, your brain doesn't know that. When you see that phantom coin floating near the top of the water, it is because your brain has created an image of the coin where the light rays *would have come from* if they had not been bent.

The Tricky Pencil

You'll need
- *a clean glass*
- *water*
- *a pencil with a flat top*

How to do the trick

Fill a clean glass with water and place it on a table. Take a pencil and stand it on the top of the table. Take a pencil and stand it on the top of the table about a foot (30cm) behind the glass. Now look through the glass of water. You'll see not one but two pencils!

Close your right eye and look through the glass of water again. You'll see only one pencil.

Open your right eye and close your left eye. How many pencils do you see this time?

Now open both eyes, look through the glass another time, and you'll see two pencils again.

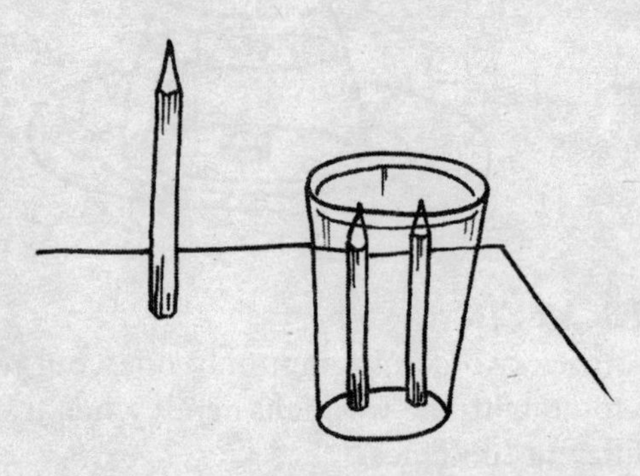

How the trick works

Because the glass is shaped like a cylinder, each eye looks through the water at a slightly different angle. So, when you have both eyes open, each eye sees a slightly different image of the pencil—and you see two pencils. When you have only one eye open, you see only one image of the pencil.

The Mystery of the Shadowy Hand and the Disappearing Finger

Check out this simple trick that befuddles your eyes and brain into seeing images that aren't really there.

How to do the trick

Hold your left hand up at arm's length in front of your face while you focus on an object about three or four feet (1m–1.2m) away. Part of a shadowy hand will appear just to the right of your left hand.

Now, still looking at the object with your left hand out in front of you, raise your right hand, extending your index finger closer and closer to your left hand, until your fingertip disappears behind it. But is your finger really hidden behind that hand? Look at your hands and see. You'll find

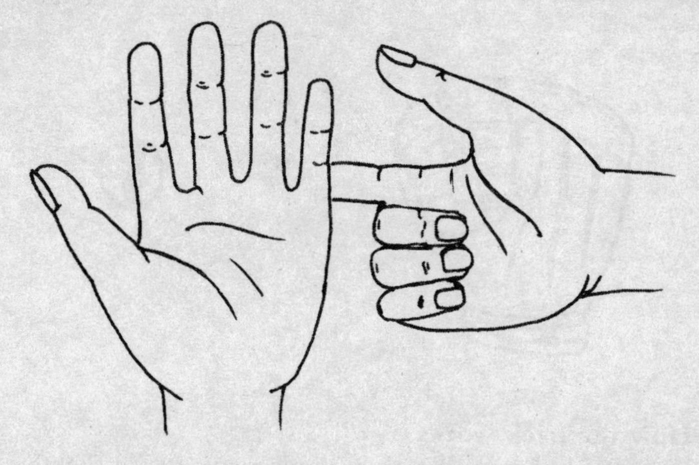

that you haven't really moved your right index finger behind your left hand—it only looks that way when you focus on the distant point. In reality, your finger will still be about half an inch (1.25cm) away from your left hand!

How the trick works

When you focus on a point about four feet (1.2m) away, the image of your hand and finger (which are only a short distance from you) becomes blurry. When you bring your index finger closer toward your left hand, the images from your right eye and your left eye overlap. As a result, your fingertip seems to disappear.

The Big Catch

How to do the trick

Pick up this book and hold it so that your nose touches the dot between the baseball and the mitt. Now, turn the book slowly in a counterclockwise direction. You will see the ball fly up in a graceful arc and land in the mitt! Congratulations! You made the big catch!

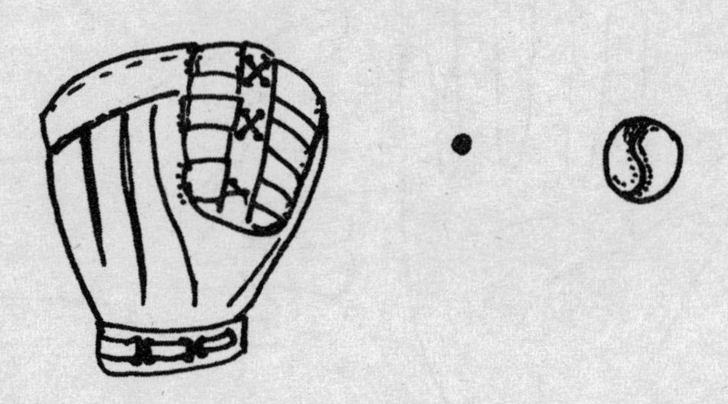

How the trick works

You already know that each of your eyes sees a slightly different picture. Close your right eye and focus on an object about three feet (1m) away from you, such as a clock or a poster. Now, quickly open your right eye and close your left. The object you're looking at will seem to change its position slightly—it may even seem to jump. Then close your right eye and open your left eye again. The object will appear to be in the same place as before.

So, now you've seen for yourself how you see a slightly different image with each eye. When you look at an object with both eyes at the same time, your brain processes both images into a single picture. When you look at the picture of the baseball and the mitt, your left eye sees the mitt, and your right eye sees the ball. When your brain combines these two images, the ball appears to sail into the mitt.

Make the Ball Disappear

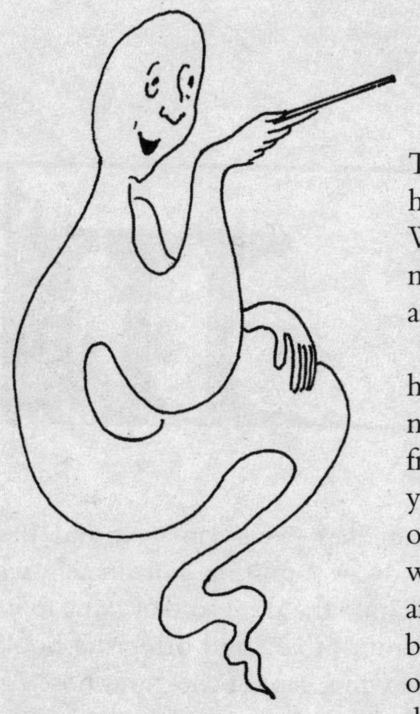

The little ghost fancies himself as a magician. With your help, he will make the ball disappear, and then appear again.

All you need to do is hold this book at a normal reading distance from your face and close your left eye. Now focus on the ghost's magic wand with your right eye and very slowly move the book toward your face. At one point, the ball will disappear.

How the trick works

Doing this trick, you have actually discovered your "blind spot." That is a point at the back of each of your eyes where your optic nerve joins the retina (that screen at the back of your eye). Most of the surface of the retina is made up of cells called "rods" and "cones." These are sensitive to light and color. However, there are none of these cells at the point where your optic nerve joins the retina, so you cannot see the light rays that are reflected onto it.

In order to find the blind spot at the back of your right eye, redraw this picture so that the ghost is on the right-hand side of the ball and repeat the experiment with your right eye closed, staring at the magic wand with your left eye as you slowly bring the page closer to your face.

Rebuild the Bridge

The bridge in the picture has been damaged and the middle section of the roadway is missing. Fortunately, it's very simple to repair. Just hold the page so that the gap in the bridge is directly in front of you and bring the book toward your face until the white gap touches your nose. At one point, the gap will close.

This illusion relies on one important fact for its success. That is, when you look at something with both eyes open, you actually see two images of the object. Your brain puts them together and interprets them as a single object.

How big or small that object seems to be depends on how far away from you it is. A person who is a long distance away might appear as small as an ant, even though that same person, if he were standing beside you, might be bigger and taller than you are.

When you slowly bring the page of this book closer to your face, the image formed by each eye gradually gets bigger. Eventually, each image is so large that the two pictures overlap and the bridge seems—mysteriously—to repair itself.

You can prove to yourself that the two images produced by your eyes rebuild the bridge. Just close one eye and bring the book closer and closer to your face until it touches your nose. Instead of seeing the two halves of the bridge meet, you'll just see one side of the bridge—and your nose!

Creating Rainbows

There is more than one way to create a rainbow, depending on the weather, the time of day, and the equipment on hand.

How to do the trick

1. On a bright, sunny day, try the following technique:

You'll need

- *a bowl*
- *water*
- *a small, flat mirror*
- *a piece of cardboard*

First, fill the bowl with water. Then take the mirror and rest it inside the bowl. Place the bowl and mirror in front of a window, or in some other place where rays of sunlight will strike the mirror. Hold the cardboard in front of the mirror, moving it around until a rainbow appears on it.

If you can't see a rainbow, adjust the position of the mirror. With a little trial and error, you'll soon create a rainbow inside your own home.

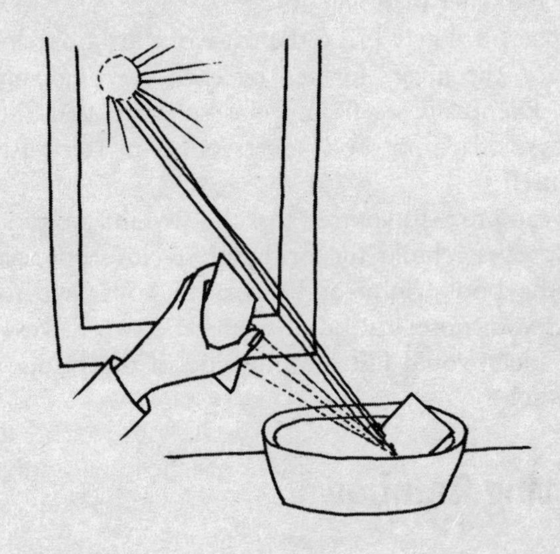

2. When the sun is low in the sky, in the morning or evening, you can make a rainbow using the following method.

You'll need
- *a glass with smooth sides*
- *water*
- *a piece of white paper*

Find a window that has sunlight streaming through it, and place the glass nearby so that the sun shines through it. You could place it on a windowsill, on a table or on a chair. Fill the glass completely full of water, and then put a sheet of white paper on the floor beneath it. A rainbow will appear on the paper.

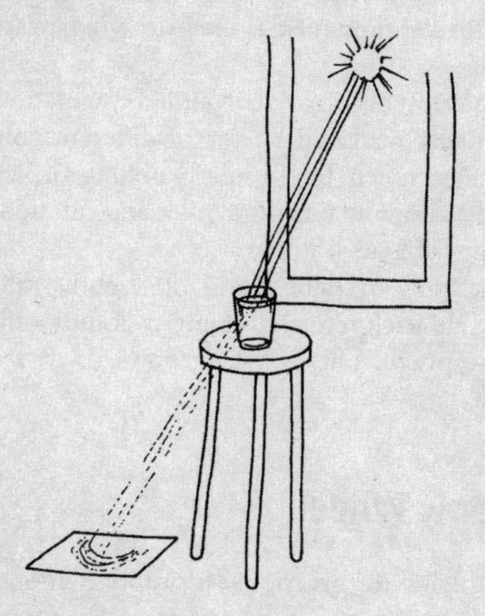

3. A third way that you can create a rainbow during the early morning or late afternoon is with a garden hose outside in the garden. Turn on the hose and adjust the nozzle, or put your thumb over the end of the hose, so that the water comes out in a spray of very fine droplets. Now stand in front of some dark shrubs with your back to the sun and you'll see a rainbow.

How these tricks work

In nature, a rainbow is created when sunlight strikes tiny droplets of water that are suspended in the air. These drops act like prisms and split the sunlight into the individual colors that make up the white light.

When you create your own rainbow using the first method, the water acts as a prism.

In the second experiment, the rim of the glass of water acts as a prism.

In the third experiment, the droplets of water act as a prism to split up the light, just as they do when you see a rainbow in the sky.

All these experiments prove that sunlight, which we see as white, is actually made up of rays of different colors—red, orange, yellow, green, blue, indigo (a blue-purple), and violet. (Sunlight also contains ultraviolet and infrared rays, but these are invisible to humans.)

All of these rays of light travel at slightly different speeds, so they are each refracted (bent) a slightly different amount by the prism. This is what allows us to see the separate colors.

The Rainbow Wheel

There's no real trick to this trick—it simply demonstrates that white light is made up of the seven colors of the rainbow. It's a fascinating thing to see, though, so we've included it in this book as part of the magic of everyday life that we take for granted.

You'll need

- *scissors*
- *a piece of cardboard*
- *a protractor*
- *colored pencils, crayons, or paint*
- *a sharp pencil*

How to do this trick

Take scissors and cut out a circle with a diameter of about four inches (10cm) from the cardboard. Then, with the protractor, divide the circle up into seven equal sections. Each section will be about 51° wide.

Color each section with one of the colors of the rainbow so that your cardboard disc looks like this:

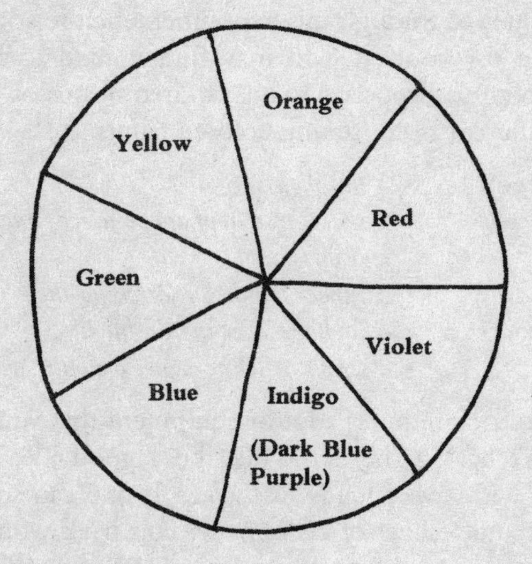

Then make a small hole in the middle of the disc and push a sharp pencil through it.

Finally, spin the pencil quickly on a hard surface so that the disc moves very rapidly. You see WHITE! Isn't it amazing?

Colored Lights

When you read through this experiment, before you actually try it for yourself, you may find it hard to believe what's going to happen. Mixing colored beams of light is totally different from mixing colored paints.

You'll need
- *3 flashlights*
- *3 sheets of cellophane, one red, one blue, and one green*
- *3 rubber bands for fastening the cellophane over the flashlights*
- *a screen or white paper or white wall*

Since this trick requires a lot of equipment that you probably don't have at home, it may be a good idea to get together with two friends so that each one can supply a flashlight and a sheet of cellophane. This trick would also make a really neat group science project for school.

How to do this trick
First, fasten a piece of cellophane over the light end of each one of the flashlights with the rubber bands. You will now have flashlights that give out red, blue, and green light.

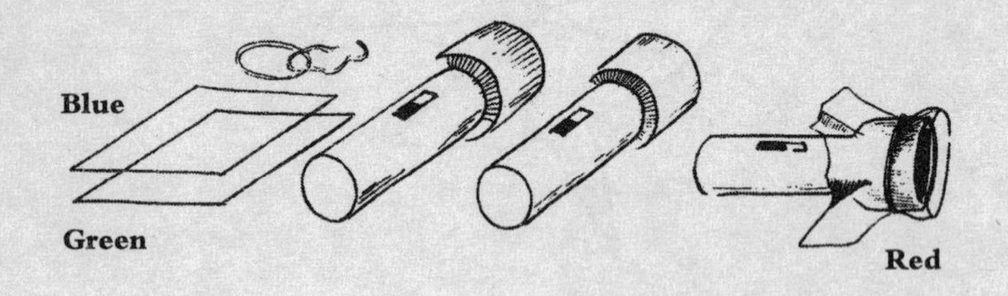

Next, find a suitable room to perform this experiment in. It should be as dark as possible. Put a blanket over the windows, if necessary. If the room has white walls you can shine your flashlight right at the wall. If not, you may need to use white paper or a movie screen if you have one.

Begin your light show by shining the flashlight with the red cellophane and the one with the blue cellophane at different places on the white wall.

Now direct the flashlight beams on the middle of the wall, so that the two beams of light overlap. The purple color that you will see is called magenta. You may have seen this color using the "paint box" of a computer.

Next, shine the blue and green beams so that they overlap. The blue-green color that you will see is called cyan. This is another color that you may have seen on a computer screen.

Now shine the red and green beams together. What color do you see? SURPRISE! I bet you didn't expect that red and green flashlight beams would combine to make yellow!

Finally, shine the flashlights at the screen so that the three different colors all overlap. What color do you see in the middle of the pool of light? You'll probably be very surprised to see that the area where all three colored beams of light overlap is actually white!

How the trick works

Red, blue, and green are known as the primary colors of light. Yes, that's different from paint, where the primary colors are red, blue, and yellow.

Magenta, cyan, and yellow—the colors that you see when you "mix" the primary colors together two by two—are known as the secondary colors of light.

All these colors have light waves that travel at slightly different speeds. When blue, red, and green lights are mixed all together, their separate wavelengths combine to form white light.

Make a Color-Viewing Box

When is a green apple no longer a green apple? When does a juicy red tomato no longer look red? When you view them through a viewing box with a red filter, of course.

You'll need

- *a shoebox (or a similar cardboard box with a lid)*
- *scissors*
- *extra cardboard*
- *sticky tape*
- *cellophane (red, green, and blue)*
- *a green apple*
- *a red tomato*

How to do this trick

The first thing you need to do is construct the viewing box. Cut a small hole, about 1½ inches (3.75cm) in diameter, in one of the narrow ends of the box. This is your viewing hole.

Next, cut a rectangular hole in the middle of the lid of the box. This hole should be about 3½ inches (8.75cm) long and 2½ inches (6.25cm) wide.

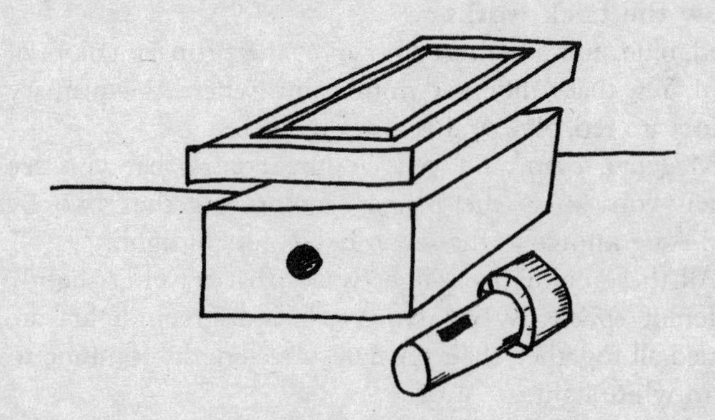

Finally, make the color filters. Cut rectangular frames out of the cardboard and tape a piece of cellophane across each one. The frames should be about four inches (10cm) long by three inches (7.5cm) wide so that they cover the hole in the top of the box. Use the red, blue, and green cellophane to make the filters.

To use your viewing box, first place the object you are going to look at in the box underneath the color filter. Then look through the viewing hole at the end of the box while you shine a flashlight through the colored filter at the top of the box.

When you look at the green apple while shining your flashlight through the red filter, it will look dark. When you look at the red tomato, it will appear pale.

How the trick works

The red filter on top of the box allows only red light rays to enter the box. The red tomato appears pale because it can reflect only the red light that passes through the filter.

As for the apple, the red filter prevents green light from entering the viewing box. Since the green apple reflects mostly green light rays, it appears dark.

When all the colored wavelengths of light are kept out, the interior of the box becomes much dimmer. This fact is important because the cone-shaped cells in the retina, which are sensitive to color, work best in bright light.

You may have noticed that in a dark room, you can't see color at all: everything you see is in shades of grey. Or you may have walked into a dim room and noticed that normally bright colors appear pale. This is what happens when you look at the red tomato when it's under the red filter. It appears pale because the dimness of the red light in the box prevents the cones in your retina from responding fully.

As for the apple, the red filter on the top of the viewing box prevents green light from entering the box, and since the green apple cannot reflect the red light, it appears dark.

Make a 3-D Viewer

Two-dimensional images drawn on a flat piece of paper can look as if they are three-dimensional with this simple 3-D viewer.

You'll need

- *a piece of paper or cardboard*
- *a ruler*
- *scissors*
- *a picture or photo*

How to make the viewer

Draw a cross in the middle of the cardboard. The vertical part of the cross should be about 2 inches (5cm) high and half an inch (1.25cm) wide. Each arm of the cross should be about ¾ of an inch (2cm) long and half an inch (1.25cm) wide.

Using a ruler, make sure that the lines are neatly drawn. Then, with scissors, cut out the cross and remove it, leaving a window in the piece of cardboard.

Next, place the picture or photo that you want to view flat on a table. Pictures of objects with lots of straight lines, such as buildings, work best. Place the cardboard upright at right angles to the picture.

Now stare down hard through the cross for a few seconds and you'll see the picture stand out in three dimensions.

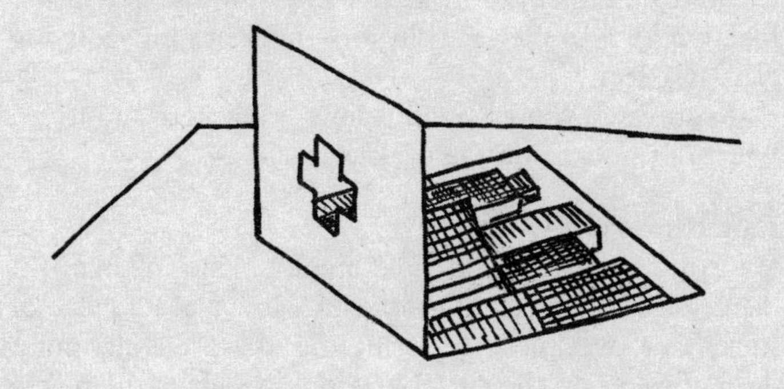

How the trick works
First, the cross hides the edges of the picture, keeping you from seeing that it's really flat. Second, your brain is used to seeing the world in three dimensions, so it automatically creates a three-dimensional image for you. We really do see what we expect to see!

Make Your Own Magnifying Glass

Challenge your friends with this simple scientific trick.

You'll need

- *a straw*
- *a small piece of cardboard*
- *a cup of water*
- *scissors*
- *clear sticky tape*
- *a sheet of newspaper*

How to do the trick

Place all the materials on a table and challenge your friends to use them to make the letters on the newspaper look bigger than they actually are—to create a magnifying glass, in effect.

If you want, you can stop reading right here and try to figure out how to do the trick yourself.

How the trick works

With the scissors, cut a circle about an inch (2.5cm) in diameter in the piece of cardboard. Now place a piece of sticky tape over the hole. Using the straw, carefully put a drop of water on the tape. Now look closely at the newspaper through the drop of water. You'll see that the letters do look bigger. You have made your own personal magnifying glass!

When you look at an object through a drop of water, it will look bigger than it really is. That's because the drop of water acts as a lens, a convex lens. A convex lens is thicker in the middle and thinner at the edges—it bulges out. A convex lens refracts (bends) light waves so that objects seems to be bigger than they actually are.

2. illusion Magic

The Disappearing Scarf

This is a fun little trick in which you show your audience an ordinary silk scarf and a paper bag. Then you blow a few breaths of air into the paper bag until it looks like a balloon. Then you burst the paper bag. Incredibly, the scarf inside doesn't fall out of the bag—it has mysteriously disappeared!

You'll need

- *a silk scarf or a large handkerchief that can be crumpled easily into a small ball*
- *2 paper bags*
- *scissors*
- *glue*

How to do the trick

First you need to make a special paper bag with a secret compartment. You need two paper bags to do it. Take a scissors and cut the bottom third off one of the paper bags, as in #1. Glue this false bottom onto one side of the inside of the other paper bag (#2). Wait for the glue to dry and you'll be ready to do the trick.

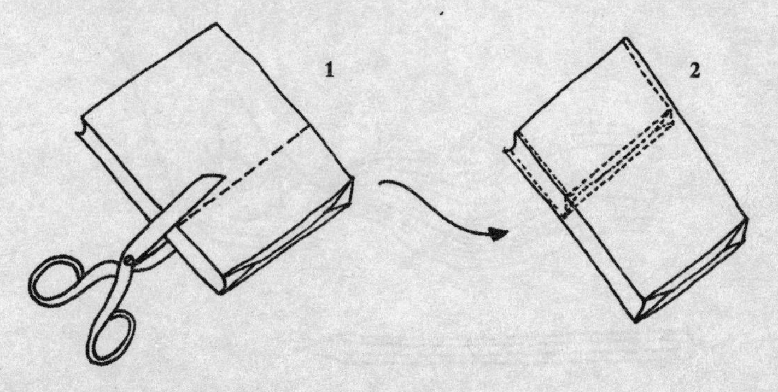

When you perform this trick, open the paper bag so that your audience cannot see inside it. Then blow gently into it to inflate it. When you take the silk scarf out of your pocket, put it into the secret compartment at the top of the paper bag (#3). Blow into the bag a few more times until it is fully inflated. Then burst the bag and listen to your audience gasp when they discover that the scarf has disappeared!

The Rubber Pencil

The Effect

You take a pencil out of your pocket and, holding it firmly in both hands, explain to your audience that this is a very weird pencil that sometimes does strange and unpredictable things. Then you take one hand off the pencil so that you are holding it by only one end. You give the pencil a few quick jerks. Suddenly, as if jolted into life, the pencil begins to bend and wiggle as if it were made of rubber.

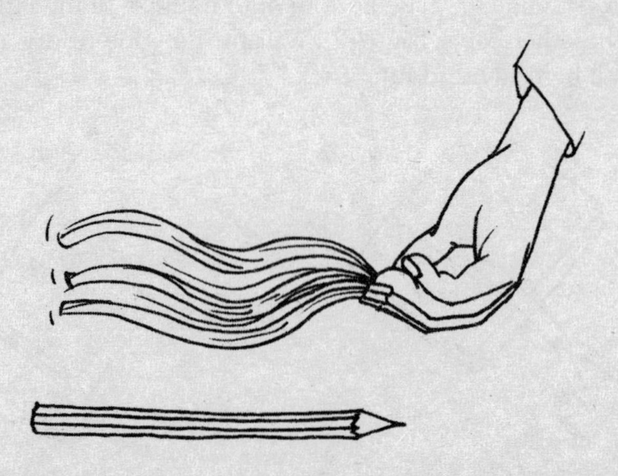

How to do the trick

The pencil that you use in this trick is just an ordinary pencil. To make it look as if it's made of rubber, simply grasp it with your right thumb and first finger, and, holding it horizontally, wiggle it with short, quick shakes. It will appear to bend without your having to do anything "magical."

How the trick works

You can move the pencil faster than the people in the audience can see it. You'll remember that, in order for you to see anything, light waves from the object first have to travel through your eye until they hit the screen at the back of your eye called the retina. The cells of the retina respond to the light waves and send a message along the optic nerve to your brain. Your brain then interprets the visual information from both eyes into a single picture of whatever it is you are looking at. The brain is able to process many of these images every second, so that you get a smooth, uninterrupted flow of vision. However, the brain cannot process these images fast enough to keep up with your wiggling pencil! It is just wiggling too fast!

So when your friends look at the wiggling pencil, instead of seeing a single image of the pencil every time it moves a tiny bit up or down in the air, they see the many possible positions of the pencil, all combined into a blurry set of images.

You've probably noticed this before when you watched the blades of an electric fan or the propeller of a plane.

Sticky Water

Who ever heard of water that sticks to the sides of a bottle and doesn't come out, even if the bottle is held upside down? No, there isn't a top on the bottle. I'll bet you've never seen this, and probably none of your friends will have either—until you show them this amazing trick that defies the force of gravity!

The Effect

You show your audience a small glass soft-drink bottle about ¾ full of water. Next, you tell them that if you put exactly the right amount of water in a bottle, it will not pour out.

Your friends watch as you hold the bottle upside down with your right hand and drops of water spill out over your left hand and into the bowl below. Suddenly, they realize that there is no more water trickling out of the bottle, and there's nothing to hold it in there either! It's as if the water has suddenly gotten sticky and is stuck to the sides of the bottle.

"There, you see?" you say.

Then, as your friends sit spellbound, you suddenly hit the bottom of the bottle with your left hand, and the rest of the water pours out into the bowl below.

You'll need

- *scissors*
- *a sheet of cellophane*
- *glass soft-drink bottle*
- *pencil (optional)*

How to do the trick

With the scissors, cut a disc in the cellophane that is the same size as the mouth of the soft-drink bottle. When you perform the trick, have this disc lying on your table beside the bottle. (You could also moisten the disc with water and stick it on the fingers of your left hand in advance.)

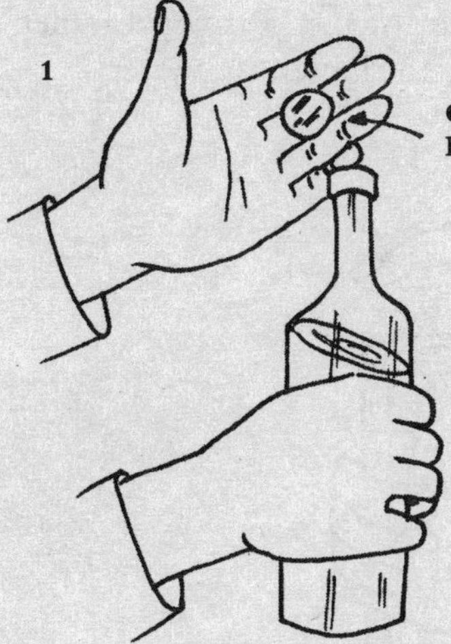

While you are still holding the bottle right-side up, slide the disc over the mouth of the bottle with the fingers of your left hand (#1).

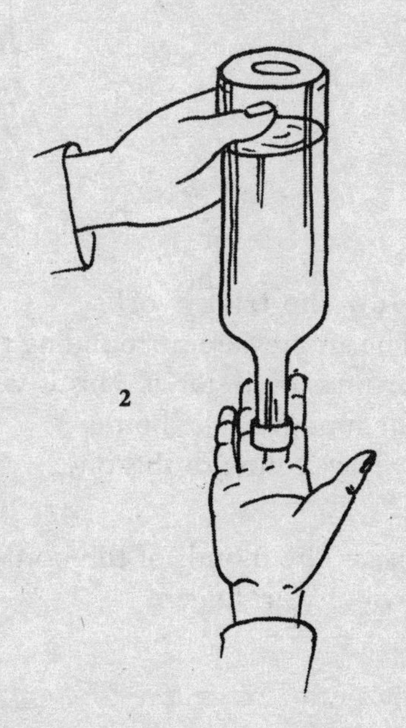

When you turn the bottle upside down, spread the fingers of your left hand very carefully, and smooth the cellophane over the mouth of the bottle. The edges of the disc will seal themselves against the bottle (#2).

When you remove your fingers, the cellophane will hold the water in place.

After your audience has had a good look at the bottle of sticky water, hit the bottom of the bottle to dislodge the disc and let the water pour out (#3). Or, if you'd rather, poke a pencil inside the bottle to "loosen the water."

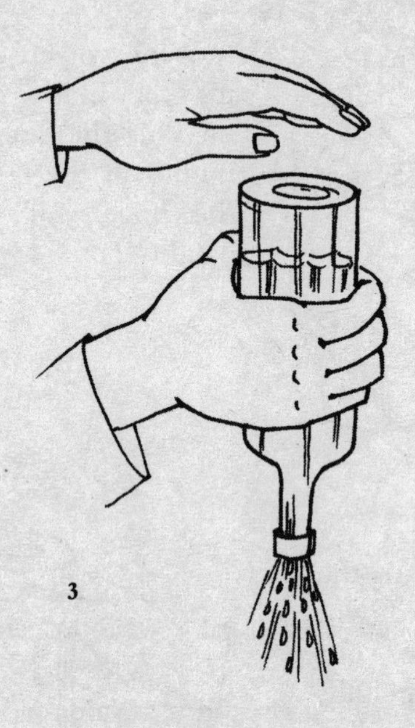

3

How the trick works

The air pressure surrounding the bottle is greater than the air pressure inside it. This is what holds the cellophane to the mouth of the bottle.

Have fun with this one!

Note: The mouth of the bottle should not be wider than two of your fingers.

3. Tactile illusions

The Muller-Lyer illusion

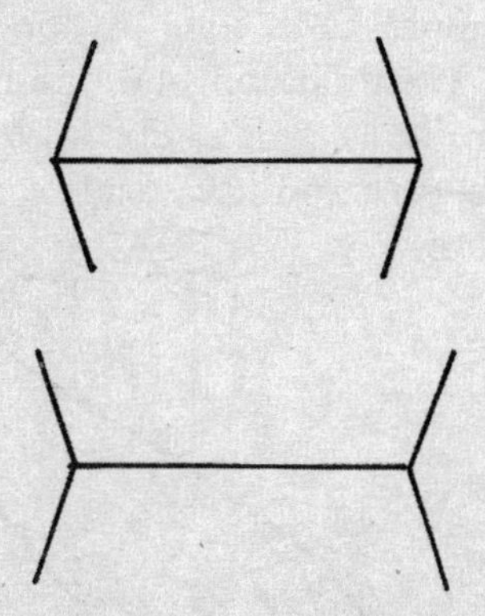

Which of these two lines do you think is longer? If you were to take a guess, you'd probably choose the bottom line. However, you'd be wrong. The bottom line does look longer, but, in actual fact, both horizontal lines are exactly the same length.

This illusion was named after the two men who discovered it, and it is one of the most puzzling of all the illusions, because it is not only an optical illusion, but it also works on a tactile level—the level of touch.

To prove to yourself that your sense of touch can be fooled by this remarkable illusion, you need to construct the object below.

You'll need
- *thick, stiff cardboard (not the corrugated kind)*
- *strong glue (paste or glue sticks are not good enough)*
- *scissors*

Begin by cutting a strip of cardboard twice as long as one of the horizontal lines in the illusion above. This strip of cardboard should be one inch (2.5cm) wide. Do this as accurately as you can. Then cut six smaller pieces of cardboard to form the "arrows" on the end of each part of the line. These should be as long as one side of the arrow shown in the visual illusion, and one inch (2.5cm) wide. Glue these small pieces of cardboard onto the long piece of cardboard so that you have made something that looks like the object below.

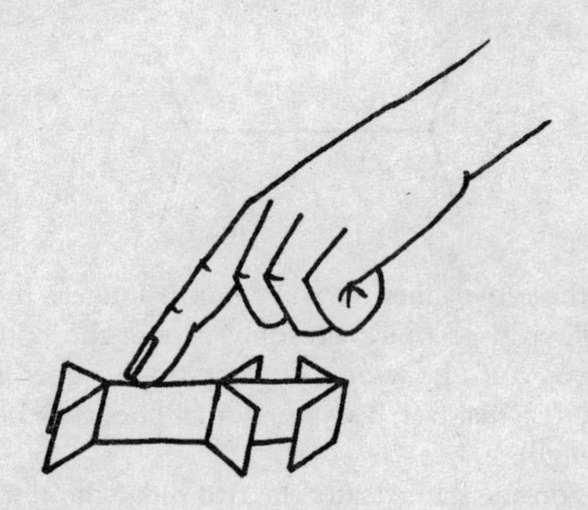

Check carefully to make sure that the angles formed by the "V" of each of the arrows are all the same size. Remember also to check that the "arrows" placed in the middle of the figure are exactly in the middle.

Then leave the object to dry.

When the cardboard illusion is completely dry, explore and compare the two parts. You'll find that your fingers come to the same conclusion that your eyes do: the section of the puzzle that has the arrows pointing inward seems to be longer than the other section of the puzzle.

How the trick works

One explanation of why the Muller-Lyer illusion works visually has been proposed by Richard Gregory, who published the results of his work on illusions in the 1970s. Using special tests for estimating distance, Gregory found that observers see the lines as symbolic of other objects. To see for yourself how Gregory came to this conclusion, turn this book around so that the straight lines are vertical. You will see that the line with the arrows pointing outward resembles a corner of the outside of a building. The line with the arrows pointing inward looks like the distant inside corner of a room. Since the vertical line of the room appears to be farther away, your visual system assumes that the line is longer than it appears to be, in order to compensate for its being in the distance.

However, this doesn't explain why the illusion works when the lines are horizontal, and it doesn't explain why the tactile illusion works.

Another theory about the Muller-Lyer illusion is the "eye movements" theory. It goes like this: when you look at the lines at the top of page 31, the bottom line seems longer because your eyes have to scan beyond the ends of the straight line in order to see the whole figure—including the arrows at the end. So your eyes have to scan a greater horizontal distance. It may be that the tactile illusion works in a similar way. Your fingers have to reach beyond the length of the straight line between the two arrows in order to touch all of this section of the puzzle. This may give us an exaggerated sense of the length of this part of the object.

Hot and Cold Water

One of the best parts of this trick is the surprise, so when you try it out on your friends, don't tell them what's going to happen.

How to do the trick

First, find three bowls or pots that are large enough for you to put your hands in. Fill the first bowl with cold water straight from the tap. Fill the second bowl with hot water—as hot as a hot bath, but no hotter. Fill the third bowl with lukewarm water—water that feels neither hot nor cold.

Place one hand in the bowl of cold water and one hand in the bowl of hot water for one minute. When the minute is up, remove your hands from both the bowls and put them in the bowl of lukewarm water. When you do this, you will experience an amazing effect. The hand that was soaking in cold water will now feel hot!

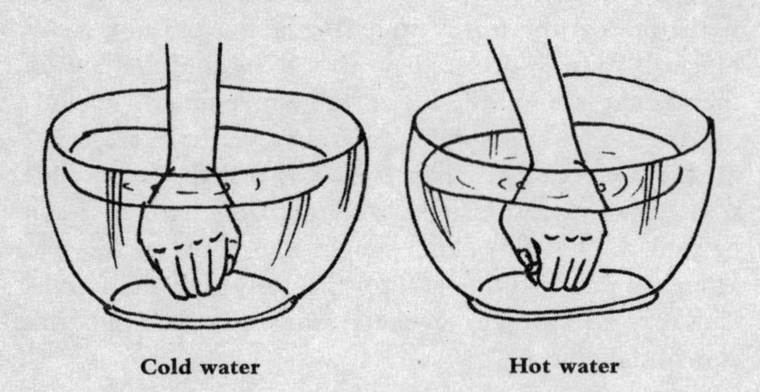

How the trick works

It works because your sense of touch relies on comparing things in order to figure them out.

If, for example, you have never slept on anything but a soft, mushy bed, a bed that is rated "medium" might seem hard to you. However, that same bed might seem soft to another person who has always slept on a firm bed. So, to the hand that was soaking in the hot water, the lukewarm water seems so much colder that your hand sends a message to your brain saying that it's cold. And to the hand that was soaking in the cold water, the lukewarm water feels so nice and warm by contrast that it sends your brain a message saying that it's hot.

That's why each of your hands tells you that the same bowl of lukewarm water is hot and cold.

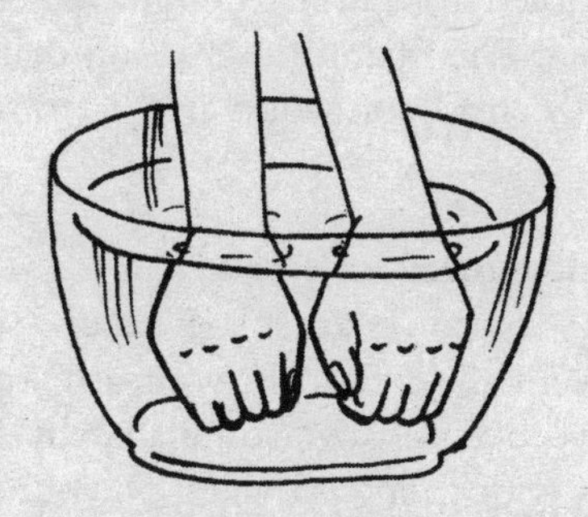

Warm water

Where Now?

This amazing trick shows that your sense of touch can be confused as easily as your sense of sight. Try this out with a friend.

Ask your friend to close her eyes and extend her bare right arm in front of her, palm up. Next, ask her to touch the back of her elbow with her left hand. Even with her eyes closed, she should have no trouble finding this spot. Now, tell your friend that you are going to touch her arm, starting at her wrist and gradually moving up toward the elbow crease. Ask her to tell you when she thinks you've reached the crease in her elbow.

Using just one finger, lightly trace overlapping circles that travel up your friend's arm. Move your finger a little more closely as you approach the crease in her elbow. She will probably tell you that you have reached the crease while your finger is still an inch or two away from it. When she does, ask her to open her eyes and see where your finger actually is. She will be amazed!

Ask your friend to try the trick on you afterwards. You'll probably be fooled too, even though you know what's going to happen! The phantom sensation that your friend is touching the crease on your arm is too real not to believe!

How the trick works

That phantom sensation is a result of "neural sensory overload"! This means the nerves in your arm that report to your brain have become overstimulated by the constant tiny circles that your friend is tracing on your arm. So they begin to tell your brain that you're being touched higher up on your arm than you actually are.

Cross Your Fingers

Here's a simple trick that is sure to amaze you and your friends.

Cross your fingers—your index finger and middle finger—just as if you were crossing them for luck, and close your eyes. Now, touch your crossed fingers to the tip of your nose. Doesn't it feel weird? Some people who do this trick report that their nose feels unusually lumpy and bumpy. Others say they have the illusion that they are touching two object, not one. Try it!

How the trick works

When you cross your fingers, the parts of your fingertips that are usually on the outside are now on the inside. The part of your skin that is touching your nose is not used to this new arrangement, and it keeps signalling to the brain that something "on the other side" is being touched. Your brain interprets this information and decides that you must either be touching two different curved surfaces or one very bumpy one!

The Curious Coin Trick

A coin is round, isn't it? Well, this trick makes you think it's oval!

First find a coin one inch (2.5cm) or more in diameter. If you don't have a large enough coin, you could use a plastic disc, such as a poker chip. Grasp the coin between the thumb and index finger of your left hand and turn it with the thumb and index finger of your right hand.

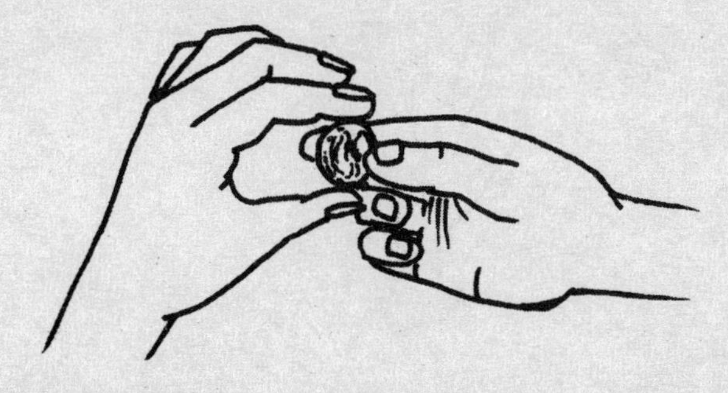

Turn the coin as quickly as you can. You'll get the strange impression that the coin is not circular, but is in fact an oval lying on its side. This illusion works best if you close your eyes.

How the trick works
It's all in the way you turn the coin. When you grasp the coin between the thumb and index finger of your right hand and rotate it, these two fingers are almost constantly in touch with the large, flat sides of the coin. This gives you a strong impression of the width of the coin.

By contrast, the height of the coin is not so clear, because the fingers of your right hand are only touching the thin edges of the coin.

Since with your eyes closed you cannot see the coin to confirm that it's really circular, your brain accepts the idea that the large, flat sides of the coin are longer than the coin is high.

That Finger Weighs a Ton!

Stretch out all the fingers of one hand, except your middle finger, which you tuck up under your hand.

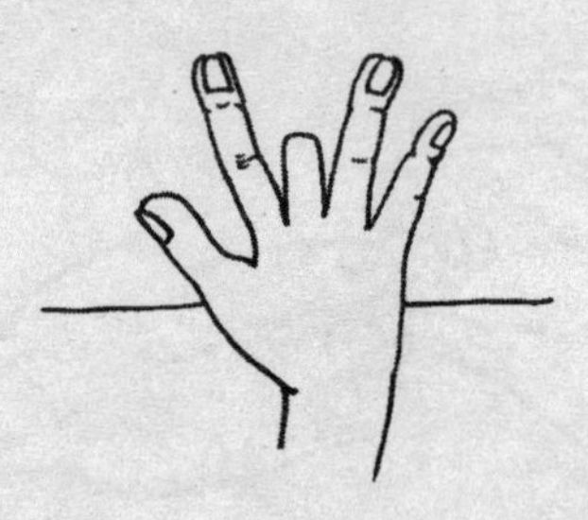

Then place your hand so that the rest of your fingertips are touching the tabletop. Now try wiggling your outstretched fingers. You'll find that you can move your thumb, your index finger, and your little finger easily, but when it comes to your ring finger, it's a different matter. For some reason, you'll find it very difficult—if not impossible—to lift it. You may experience the illusion that it is just extremely heavy, when it really weighs no more than your index finger.

How the trick works

Your middle finger and your ring finger share the same tendon, so it's very easy to bend them both at the same time. But lifting your outstretched ring finger while your middle finger is bent puts a strain on the tendon that they share.

Doing the Twist

This stunt should prove that even though you've lived with your fingers all your life, you still don't know everything about them.

How to do the trick

Hold your arms in front of you with your elbows bent and your upper arms vertical, as if you were holding a heavy bar level with your forehead. Then bring your right arm over so that your right elbow is sitting in the crook of your left elbow. Now bring your right wrist behind your left arm and clasp all your fingers together. Ask a friend to point to one of your fingers. Try to move that finger. You probably won't be able to move it the first time that you do this trick. You may think that you're moving the correct finger, but actually find that you're moving a finger on the other hand. If your friend touches the correct finger, it may help your poor, confused brain identify which finger it is supposed to move.

How the trick works

The trick works by confusing your brain. Normally, your right hand is on the right side of your body and your left hand is on the left. But when you twist your arms and fingers the way you do in this trick, nothing is normal, and your brain becomes confused.

You can see for yourself that it is the unfamiliar position that is confusing your brain by practicing the trick for a while. The longer your practice, the easier it gets to identify which finger you need to move.

The illusion of Weightlessness

If you've ever worked out in a gym, done a lot of heavy lifting, or held your arms up for a long time, you'll know what it's like to have arms that feel heavy as lead. Well, here's a trick that will convince you that your arms are lighter than even a feather.

How to do the trick

Stand in an open doorway and press your arms against the sides. Count to 60 slowly as you do this. Make sure to press outward as hard as you can. When 60 seconds have passed, step out of the doorway and into a clear space that is free of obstacles. You'll find that your arms mysteriously rise up as though pulled by some unknown force.

How the trick works

After their mighty effort pressing against the side of the door, your arm muscles have not yet had time to "switch off" and relax. So they continue to lift your arms outward and upward, after you have stepped clear of the doorway.

4. Everyday illusions

The Onion-Carrot Trick

Your senses of sight and touch are not the only ones that can be fooled. You can fool your sense of taste and smell as well. For example, you can trick your friend into thinking that she's eating a piece of onion when she's really eating a piece of carrot.

How to do the trick

While your friend is in another room, cut a very thin sliver from a fresh carrot. The cut a slice of onion.

Return to your friend and put a blindfold over her eyes. Then, hold the slice of onion underneath your friend's nose and place the the piece of carrot between her lips. Ask her to eat the food that you have place in her mouth, and to tell you what she thinks it is. She will probably reply that she thinks she's eating an onion. Then remove your friend's blindfold and show her that she has been eating a carrot all along. She will be amazed.

How the trick works

To understand how this trick works, you have to know how you taste and smell things.

When you taste something, tiny amounts of food that have been dissolved in saliva go into your taste buds—the little bumpy patches on your tongue. Inside the taste buds there are tiny little taste cells that have hairs in them. They send messages to your brain that identify what you're tasting.

When you smell something, molecules of that substance dissolve in the watery mucous at the top of the nose. The dissolved smell reaches your smell receptors, a patch of tissue full of nerve endings. They send messages to your brain that identify what you're smelling.

Your sense of smell is a lot stronger than your sense of taste. It is a vital part of enjoying the food that you eat. That's why, when you have a cold, you often find that your food loses its taste. When your friend eats the carrot thinking that it's an onion, it's because the weaker messages sent by your taste buds are masked by the more powerful messages that your smell receptors send to your brain.

Crazy Glass

Glass can bend light in some surprising ways. For instance, if you were to see a straight-haired friend standing behind a beveled glass door, you might be fooled into believing that she had just gotten her hair permed. It will look crinkly through the beveled glass because, as we saw earlier, light waves travel at different speeds through different substances and surfaces that are at different angles.

When the light waves enter or leave a substance that has different density or thickness, they bend slightly (it's refraction again). When your friend's hair looks permed, it's because the light waves have been bent at slightly different angles by the different thicknesses of glass.

What Do You Really Look Like?

When you look at your face in the mirror, you see an image that looks like you—but you don't see what you really look like. To see the same view of yourself that other people see, you have to use not one mirror but two. If you hold the first mirror in front of your face, and then hold the second mirror so that it reflects your image from the first mirror, then what you see in the second of the two mirrors is what you really look like.

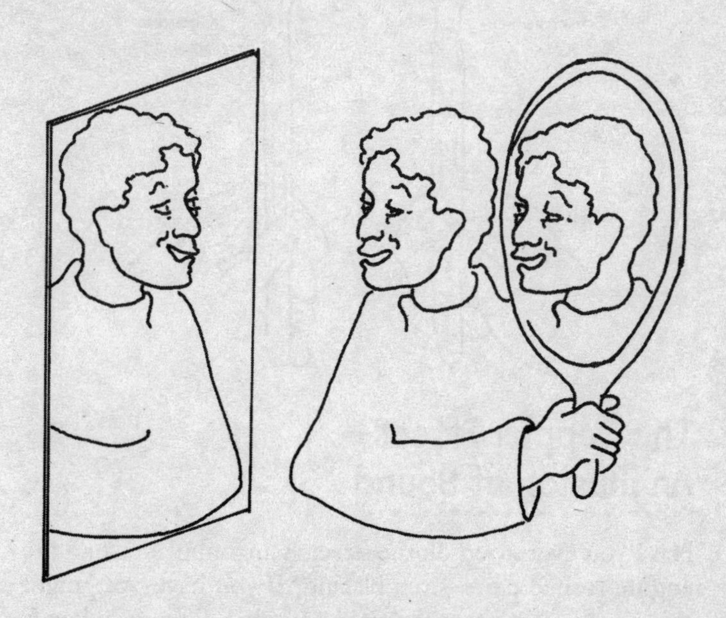

There are other images of yourself that are even less true to life than your mirror image. Hold up a shiny spoon and look into its hollow dish. Your reflection will look back at you—upside down. If you look at the other side of the spoon—the side that bulges out—you'll find that the reflection of your face also appears to bulge outward around the middle—and it's distorted in other ways, too.

Both of these images are illusions caused by the way that the light rays are bent when they strike the curved surfaces of the spoon.

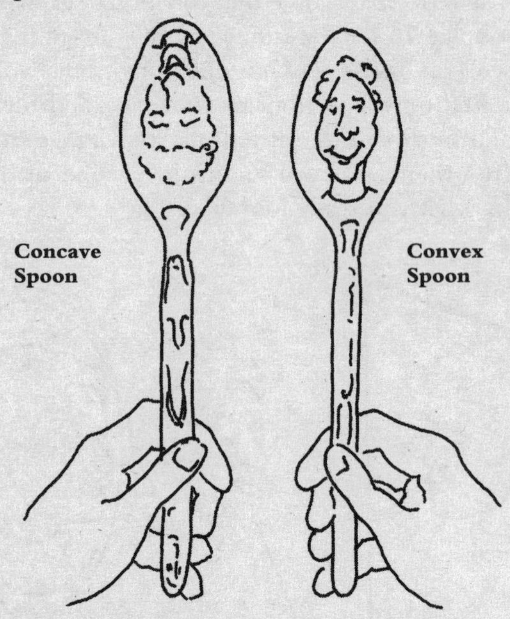

The Doppler Effect—An illusion of Sound

Have you ever stood on the street as an ambulance or a fire engine rushed past—siren blaring? If you have, you might also have noticed that the siren sounded different when it was coming toward you than it did after it passed and was speeding off into the distance. This is called the "Doppler effect."

Another example of this strange phenomenon is the way the sound of a car's engine seems to change when it approaches and then passes you at high speed. If you ever thought that the change in the car engine was due to something that the driver was doing, such as changing gears or putting his foot down hard on the gas pedal, you were wrong. The change in sound was actually a common audio illusion.

How it works

The reason why noisy things sound different when they approach than they do when they pass you has to do with the nature of sound.

Scientists describe sound as waves travelling through a substance such as air or water. There are three different factors that determine what a sound is like. These are its length, known as wavelength; how fast it's travelling, known as the speed of the wave; and how often the waves are produced, known as frequency.

When waves are produced by an engine, they spread out and travel through the air in a circular pattern, rather like the way ripples spread out around a stone you throw into still water.

If you're standing next to a parked car that has its engine running, you can think of each sound wave as a pulse of energy that travels through the air until it reaches your ears and you are able to hear it. Each wave of sound that reaches you has the same wavelength. It has the same speed and follows the previous wave after the same time interval, so the frequency of the sound waves is the same. Therefore, you hear the sound the engine makes as a constant noise.

When a car is approaching you, however, it's a different matter. The frequency of the sound waves increases. This is because when the car is moving toward you, it is also moving toward the sound waves sent off by its engine.

Imagine, for example, that a car is speeding down an empty road, its engine sending off a sound wave. By the time the engine sends off its next sound wave, the car is starting to catch up with the first sound wave. Then, by the time it sends off a third sound wave, the car is catching up with the second sound wave it produced.

As the car continues to travel toward you, this pattern continues, so that the sound waves that reach you are closer together: they arrive at a greater frequency.

When the car passes you and moves away into the distance, the opposite effect takes place. The sound waves you hear are those that spread out and travel away from the car in the opposite direction from the one the car is taking.

Imagine, now, that the car's engine sends off a sound wave that travels toward you as the car drives off into the distance. When the engine sends off the next sound wave, it will have farther to travel than the first sound wave in order to reach you. This pattern continues as the car races off into the distance. The individual sound waves that follow have farther and farther to go before they reach you, so you hear them less often. Their frequency decreases. It is this decreasing frequency of the sound waves that causes you to hear a change in the sound of the engine.

Wacky Wheels

Next time you see a cyclist pedaling by really fast, take a good look at the wheels on her bike. If you watch the spinning wheels carefully enough, you'll think they are spinning backwards! Then you will once again see them spinning forward in the direction that the bike is travelling.

How the illusion works

The reason that the bicycle wheels sometimes appear to be spinning backwards is really quite simple. It's because they're revolving so quickly that your visual system just can't keep track of what they're doing.

Your eyes and brain can only process a certain number of images each second. They can't really cope with any more information.

In the case of the spinning bicycle wheels, your brain stops trying to follow the forward motion of the spokes and starts following how many complete revolutions the wheels make instead.

When the spinning bicycle wheels don't appear to complete a full circle (a 360° revolution), your brain interprets any shortfall as backwards motion.

Which Way?

When you're travelling in a car at high speeds on a highway, you might come across this peculiar illusion.

If you sit in the backseat of the car and look out the side windows, you can experience the very strong feeling that the cars going in the opposite direction are whizzing past terrifically fast and the car that you're in isn't moving at all. It's a lot like another famous illusion: sitting in a stopped train while watching a neighboring train start up—and being sure that your train is moving.

How the illusion works

The reason that you sometimes feel as if you're not moving—although you're travelling along at a high speed—has to do with the way your brain adapts to your environment.

You've probably noticed, for example, if you visit friends who live in a noisier neighborhood than yours, that while the traffic may sound very loud to you, your friends no longer notice it. They have lived with the noise long enough to have become accustomed to it. Their brains "tune out" the noise.

A similar thing happens to sailors after they've been at sea for a while. They automatically adjust their stride to compensate for the swaying of their ship. When they first disembark, they may walk with a strange rocking motion for a while until they adjust to the fact that the land doesn't sway from side to side the way their ship does.

After you've travelled in a car for a while, your body and brain adjust to the motion of the car and tune it out, so you feel as if you're not moving. And since you feel as if you're not moving when in fact you're going 60 miles (96km) per hour, the cars going in the other direction seem to whiz by twice as fast. This is because the combined speed of both cars moving away from the point where they passed each other is 120 miles (192km) per hour.

Ping-Pong Blank Out

For an extremely interesting way to experience how your brain "tunes out" constant stimuli, try the following experiment.

Take a Ping-Pong ball and cut it in half with scissors, making the edges as smooth as possible. Then lie down in a quiet, dim place, and put one Ping-Pong ball over each eye. Simply gaze up into the dim whiteness of the hollow shell and let your thoughts drift.

At some point, while you're staring into the Ping-Pong balls, you will probably experience what is known as "blank out"—the experience of not seeing. Your sense of sight will seem to literary disappear. You won't even be able to tell whether your eyes are open or closed!

Scientists who have studied this phenomenon report that although the visual information from the inside of the Ping-Pong balls reaches your retina, it disappears in your brain! Because the visual information never changes, your brain just ignores it.

Some people have reported that in addition to not seeing, they also experience dream-like images. After trying this experiment, you may find that you feel very relaxed. While you were in the "blank out" state, your brain waves changed from faster to slower beta waves, and to more powerful alpha waves, which are associated with relaxation and accelerated learning.

Down the Road

You may have experienced this optical illusion when you're travelled down a long, straight, flat road—or looked down a straight section of railway tracks. In both cases, even though you know that the edges of the road and the railway tracks are evenly spaced, they don't look as if they are. As you look farther off into the distance, the road or the tracks seem to get narrower and narrower. If you could see far enough, the two lines would seem to meet and the road would disappear.

How the illusion works

The reason that things in the distance seem to be smaller than things that are close to you has to do with the way that your eyes and brain calculate size.

In general, the size of the angle made between the edges of the thing that you're looking at and your eyes determines how big or small the object seems to be. The farther away the object, the smaller the angle. The closer the object, the bigger the angle.

You can test this out. Take a piece of paper and draw a horizontal line three inches (7.5cm) long at the top of the page, parallel to the top edge of the paper. Now find the center of this line and mark it with a tiny dot.

Measure two inches (5cm) down the paper from the center of the line and draw another, larger dot. This dot represents the front of your eyes.

Next, draw two lines from this dot to the ends of the horizontal line. You will have an upside-down triangle. The angle between the two slanting lines and the dot that stands for your eyes is called your "angle of vision."

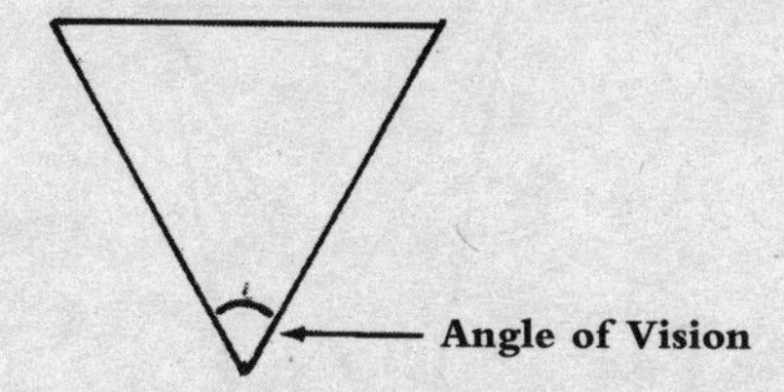

Now measure about six inches (15cm) from the horizontal line, and mark that point with another dot. This dot also represents the front of your eyes, but this time they are farther away from the horizontal line. Connect this new dot to the horizontal line to form another upside-down triangle.

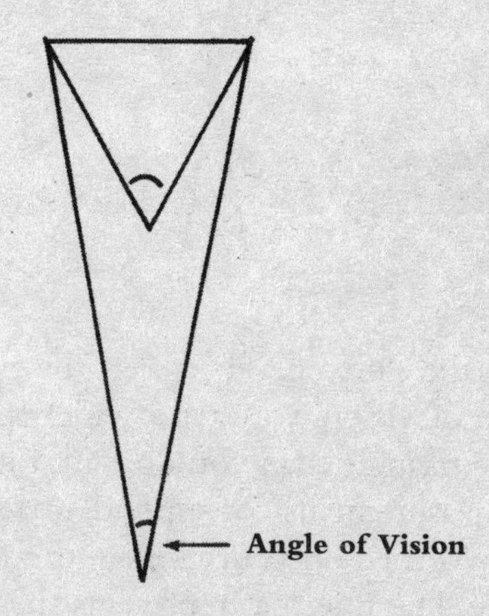

You will see that the angle formed at the bottom of this triangle is much smaller than the first angle.

Now you can see for yourself that when you look at things that are close to you, you've got a larger angle of vision than you do with things that are farther away.

Next, imagine that the lines that form the sides of the triangle cross each other when they enter your eye, so that they form an X.

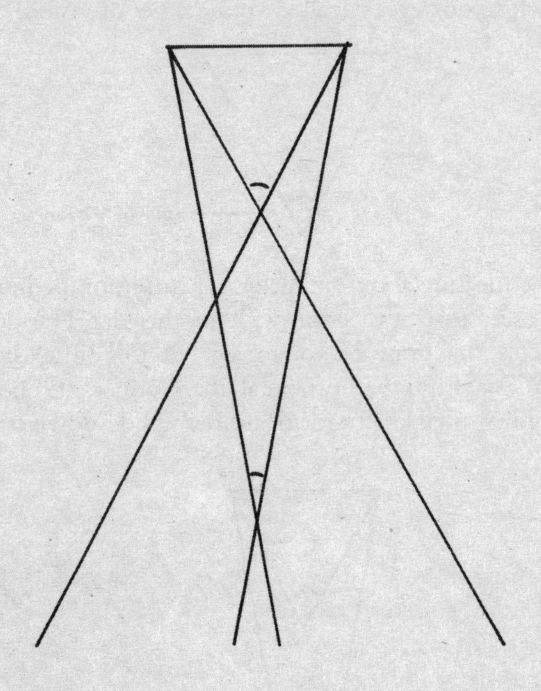

Look at the difference between the two X's. With the wide angle of vision, you get a wider space between the arms of the triangle than you do with the narrower angle.

These measurements correspond, in a simplified way, to the images formed on your retina—the screen at the back of your eye. The line that represents the closer object has a larger angle of vision—so it forms a larger image on your retina, and it looks larger to you.

Mirages

When crossing a burning hot desert, thirsty travellers often say that they can see a lake full of cool, shining water. But when they rush to the place where the lake appears to be, they find it isn't there at all. Their wonderful vision of refreshing water has been only a mirage—a natural optical illusion.

You don't have to live in the desert to see a mirage. Often on hot summer days in the city you can look down the street and see what looks like a pool of water shimmering in the middle of the road. If you take a closer look you find that the road is completely dry. The pool of water was only a mirage.

Mirages are caused by that process we talked about before called "refraction." Because light travels at different speeds through different temperatures, it actually bends from its straight line path and travels to your eye at a different angle.

When this happens, you are receiving a "false" message, and you can be fooled into thinking that the mirage is real.

5. Hidden Pictures

The picture puzzles in this section come from Cole's Funny Picture Book, a book by Edward William Cole that was published in the 1800s. Cole's book contains all sorts of stories, rhymes and funny pictures. But the most interesting things in the book are the picture puzzles, the best of which are reprinted here. These pictures may look ordinary enough, but they're really great examples of the art of illusion. If you didn't know that there were hidden pictures inside the pictures, you'd probably never know what you were missing.

For example, in this picture, some wild animals have gotten loose. Where is the bear?

So, look sharp and see just how many of the hidden faces, animals, and people you can find. If you get really stuck, you'll find the answers to the picture puzzles at the back of this book.

He's up in the tree.

This is an easy one. Usually, you'll need to turn the book around and look harder.

---

1. Here is the Showman and his learned Dog. Where is his Wife?

2. Here are the Rats. Where is the Cat?

3. Here is Bluebeard and his Wife. Where is the Donkey?

4. Here is a lot of Furniture in a Room. Where is the Cup?

5. A Giant's Castle. Where is the Giant?

6. Old Mother Hubbard. Find her Landlord.

7. Old Mother Hubbard. Find the Butler.

8. Old Mother Hubbard. Find the Doctor.

9. Mother Hubbard with a few of her children. Where are her five other children?

10. Here is the Cat. Where are the Rats?

11. This is a Newfoundland Dog. Find his Master.

12. Here is the Nurse. Where is the Patient?

13. The Falls of Niagara. Find Captain Webb.

14. The Queen is looking for His Majesty. Where is the King?

15. You can see the Goat plainly. Find the Milkmaid.

16. Here is the Cook. Where is the Rabbit?

17. Here is a Seashore. Where is the Bird?

Answers to Hidden Pictures

1. The showman's wife is actually the showman's dog. The dog's front legs form her legs, and the dog's fluffy tail forms her head.

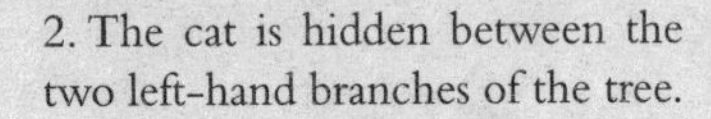

2. The cat is hidden between the two left-hand branches of the tree.

3. The donkey is hidden between the two women.

4. The table is the cup. Its handle is formed by the back of the chair on the right-hand side.

5. The houses at the top of the picture are built on top of the giant's nose. The small forest to the right forms his eyebrows. The enclosure near the middle of the picture forms his ear, and the large patch of forest forms his beard.

6. Turn the book upside down and you will see the landlord's face in what has become the far left-hand side of the picture, between the ground and the branches of the tree.

7. The butler is hidden in the dog's coat. Turn the page upside down and you will see that the dog's left-hand shoulder is also the butler's chin. The butler's nose extends under the dog's left arm.

8. The doctor's face is hidden behind the cat's back.

9. One child's face is hidden in the top of the mother's hat. Another child's face is hidden in the shoe, just above the tray that the woman is carrying. (This face is upside down.) Another child's face is hidden below the shawl that the woman wears around her shoulders, and another bulges out of the back of her apron, just below the bow tied around her waist. The face of the last child is hidden in the hem at the bottom of her apron.

10. The rats' faces are hidden in the cat's ears.

11. The dog's master is hidden in the dog's face. Turn this picture upside down and you will see that the part of the dog's ear hanging down past the far side of the dog's face forms the man's hat. The man's bearded face and hair are hidden on the lower part of the dog's face, between his nose and eye.

12. The patient is standing behind the nurse, wearing a shirt with spots on it. The patient's head is directly behind that of the nurse.

13. Captain Webb's face is hidden in the cliff at the left-hand side of the picture. The bottom of his nose is about an inch below the bottom of the two pine trees.

14. Turn the book so that the queen is lying on her front, and you will see the king's head in what is now the top right-hand corner of the picture. His arm stretches down toward the bottom of the picture, and his legs extend up to the queen's head.

15. The tree behind the goat forms the milkmaid's hair. The goat's tail and back leg form the silhouette of her nose, mouth, and chin.

16. The rabbit has hidden itself cleverly on top of the cook's head, in his hat, the last place that he would think to look for it.

17. The bird is hidden in the top left-hand portion of the picture. The bird's beak and breast are defined by the outer curves of the two baskets in the left-hand side of the drawing. The bird's eye is the little bump on the side of the stick in the top left of the drawing.

6. Shadow illusions

These shadow illusions also come from Cole's Funny Picture Book. To bring them to life, you need a blank wall and a reasonably bright, direct source of light that shines onto your hands.

It's always fun to make these fantastic shadow characters, but it's a specially good thing to do when you're sick in bed.

Once you've mastered some of the shadow illusions—or invented some of your own—you might like to put on a shadow play for your family and friends.

A good way to do this is to stretch an old white sheet across an open doorway. Turn on the light in the room in which you want to perform, and ask your audience to sit in the room on the other side of the sheet. It's best if the room in which your audience sits is dark—or only dimly lit.

To create special effects, such as the sun or a bonfire, get a friend to help by shining a flashlight with a colored filter on it (see "Colored Lights," pages 18–19).

1. Duck

2. Pig

3. Human Head

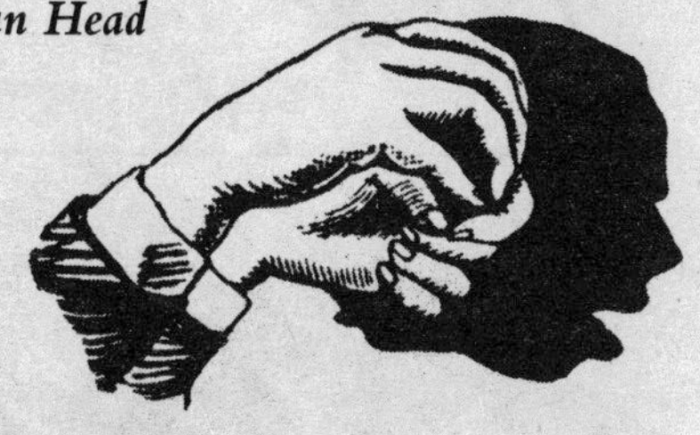

4. Rabbit

5. Evil Character

6. Goat
7. Elephant
8. Bird

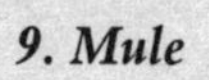

9. Mule

10. Parrot

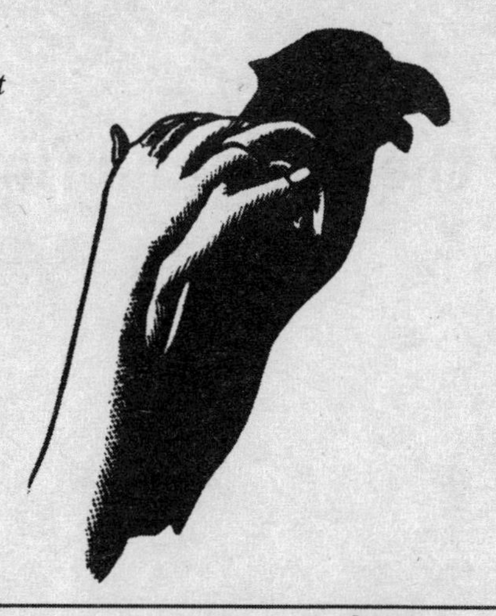

11. Dog

The middle of a book
is the end of a book?
How can that be?

FLiP the book and find out!

OPTICAL ILLUSION FLIP BOOK

AMAZING OPTICAL TRICKS

Katherine Joyce

SCHOLASTIC INC.
New York Toronto London Auckland Sydney
Mexico City New Delhi Hong Kong Buenos Aires

Line Illustrations by Angelika Echsel

ISBN 0-439-39735-9

Published by Scholastic Inc., 557 Broadway, New York, NY 10012, by arrangement with Sterling Publishing Company, Inc. SCHOLASTIC and associated logos are trademarks and/or registered trademarks of Scholastic Inc.

12 11 10 9 8 7 6 5 4 3 2 1 2 3 4 5 6 7/0

Printed in the U.S.A. 40

First Scholastic printing, April 2002

Contents

introduction

Seeing spots before you eyes? Seeing objects that don't exist? You're not crazy—you're seeing an illusion! And now you can make your very own—and amaze those around you, too! Learn how to turn one pencil into two. Make your very own 3-D viewer. And when you've fooled yourself—and your friends!—flip the book and find another! There's a whole collection of great optical illusions just waiting to astound you.

Two books in one? It's magic!

1. Optical illusion Tricks

Coin Magic

Here's an experiment you might like to try with your friends.

You'll need

- *a bowl*
- *a coin*
- *some water*

How to do the trick

Place the bowl on a table and put the coin inside it. Now, back away from the table until you can no longer see the coin. As soon as the coin has disappeared from sight, stop moving and ask a friend to pour some water into the bowl. Amazingly, you can see the coin again!

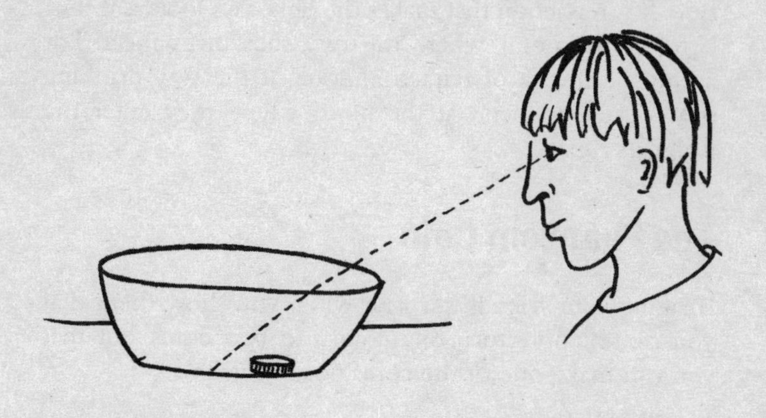

How the trick works

This trick relies on the fact that light travels more quickly through air than through water. When the light rays slow down as they enter the water, they also change direction a

little (see the diagram below). This allows you to see the coin again.

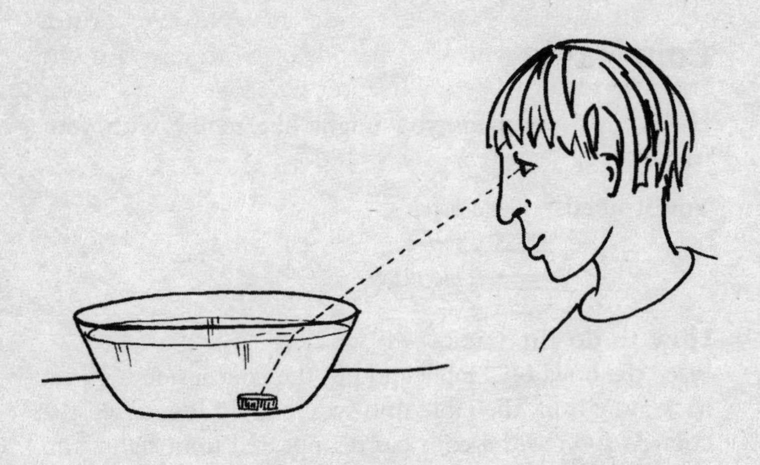

There is a special word to describe the way light appears to bend as it travels through different substances—refraction. It is refraction that makes the light rays look as if they bend at the point where the two substances meet. For another example of refraction, look at the way drinking straws seem to bend at the point where they enter the water in a glass.

The Phantom Coin

Imagine your friends' surprise when you show them that you cannot only turn one coin into two coins, but that you can make one of the coins float as well!

You'll need

- *a glass*
- *water*
- *a saucer*
- *a coin*

What I'm talking about is a very complicated phenomenon that is called **perception**. Perception is turning what we see into what we understand. Our perception is our view of the world. It's our perception that tells us the first shape looks a little like an elongated egg and the second looks like the circular wheel of a bicycle.

It's our perception that tells us that the word SUNSHINE is written here—

—when actually it isn't.

You were able to read the word SUNSHINE even though all the letters weren't written there—and they really weren't—because the black shadows made the word appear. The shadows enabled you to **perceive** the word, in the same way that these few shadows enable you to perceive the clear shape of a bird:

Usually, we see what we expect to see, but sometimes our perception lets us down and we perceive something to be so that isn't actually so!

That should happen to you quite a few times as you look through this book, because optical illusions very often manage to fool your perception and make you begin to *wonder if seeing is believing after all*!

Now You See It...

What's this?

An elegant vase or two old men?

It's both, of course. Concentrate on the white area and you'll see the vase. Concentrate on the black and the two men will appear.

Great Gaze

Gaze at the pattern on the facing page for at least a minute.

Quickly look at a perfectly blank wall and you'll find that you start seeing strange little moving specks on the wall.

It's weird, but don't let it frighten you!

Five Fields

Here are five fields.

Which is the largest and which is the smallest in area?

All five fields have exactly the same area. The different shapes make them appear to be different sizes.

Curious Cube

Look carefully at the drawing on the next page and then try to answer these three questions:

1. Is the cube on a table and you are looking at it from above?
2. Is the cube in midair and you are looking at it from below?
3. Does the line across the corner of the cube seem slightly bent?

You could be looking at the cube from above or below! Sometimes you will feel you're looking up at the cube from below and sometimes you will feel you are looking down on the cube from above.

The line does seem to be slightly bent, but it isn't. It's perfectly straight!

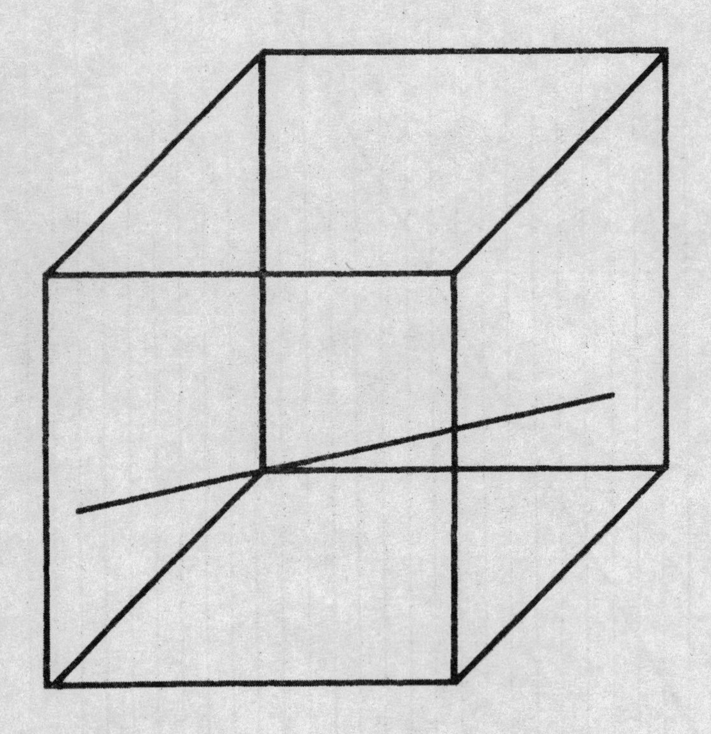

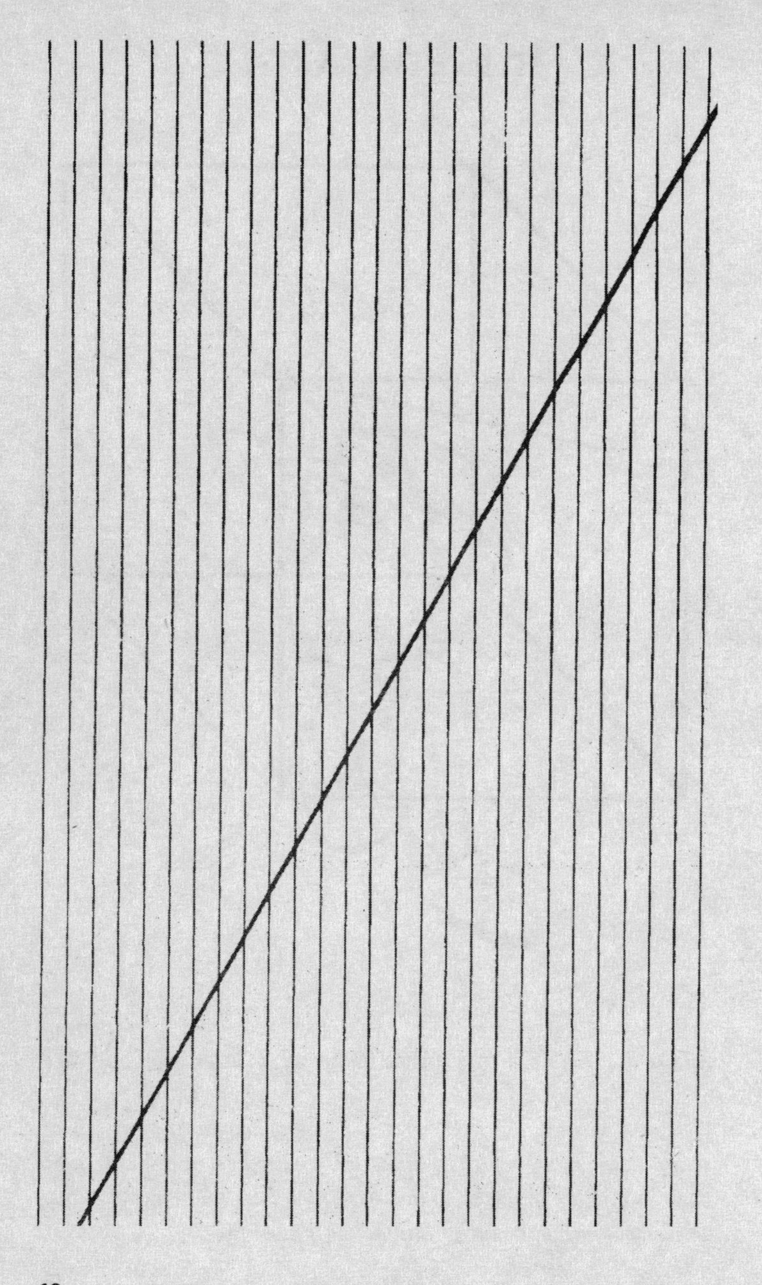

18

Ins and Outs

Look carefully at the diagonal line on the facing page.

Is it straight? Or does it twist in and out of the horizontal lines and seem a little jagged?

The diagonal line is quite straight. The vertical lines behind it make it seem distorted.

Around and Around

Look at *either* the circle on this page or the next.

Concentrate on it and revolve the book. Turn it around and around as quickly as you can.

When you stop, for a moment the pattern will suddenly seem to go around in the opposite direction.

X Marks the Spot

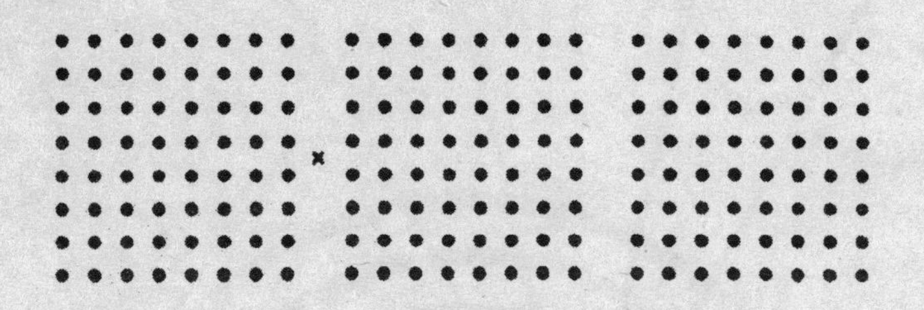

Focus on the spot marked X and you will find that the dots in the square on the left appear in horizontal **rows** while the dots in the square on the right appear in vertical **columns**.

It will always happen that way—never the other way around!

Right Angle?

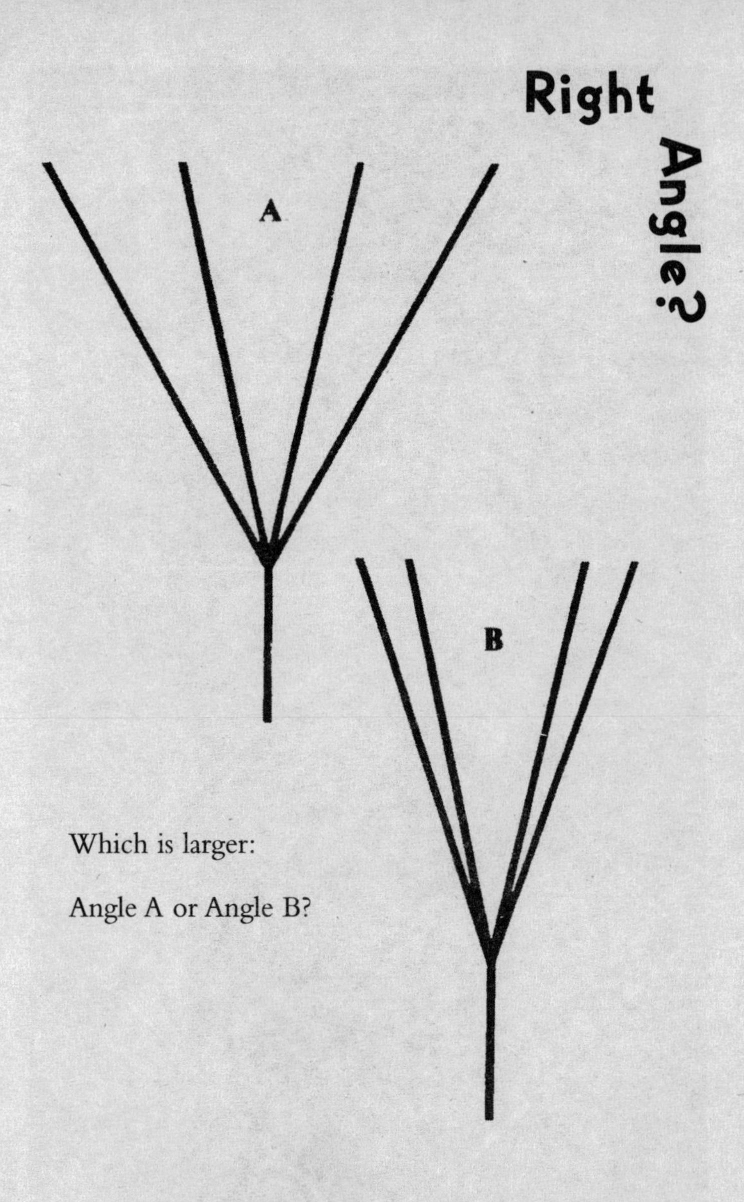

Which is larger:

Angle A or Angle B?

The angles are the same! They look unequal because of the other angles on either side of them which are different.

24

Diamonds and Squares

Which is bigger:

the diamond or the square?

They are both squares and are the same size, but a square will seem larger when tilted on one side and viewed like a diamond.

Eye Dazzler

Look at the facing page for long enough and your mind will really begin to boggle.

What can you see? Rows of triangles? Rows of squares? Rows of open boxes seen from above? Or a mixture of different patterns that keep changing as you look at them?

Far Out

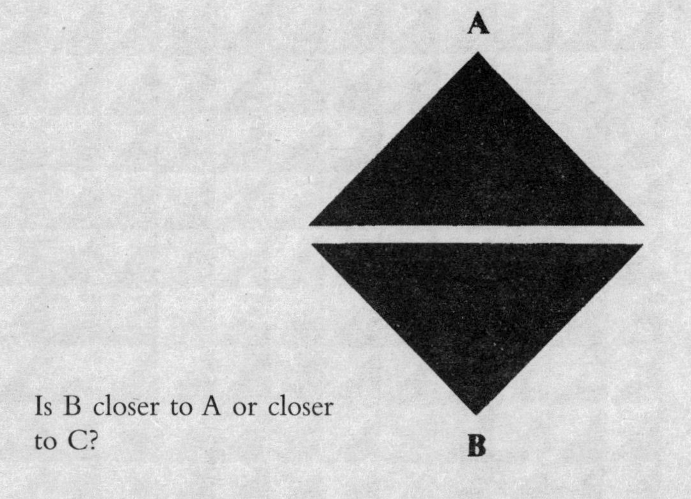

Is B closer to A or closer to C?

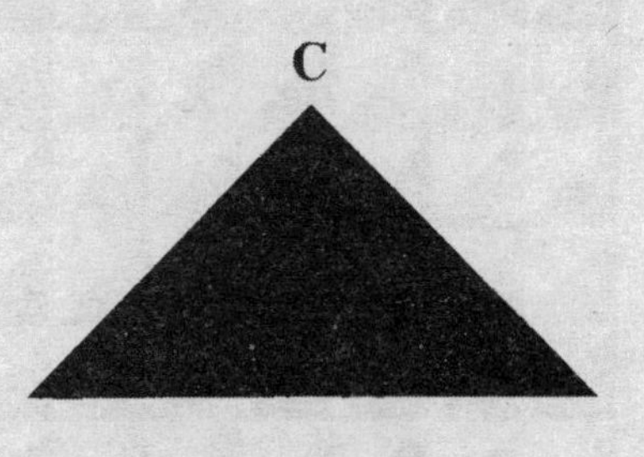

B looks a lot closer to A, doesn't it? In fact, B is exactly mid-way between A and C, so the distance between A and B and B and C is identical.

Seeing Circles

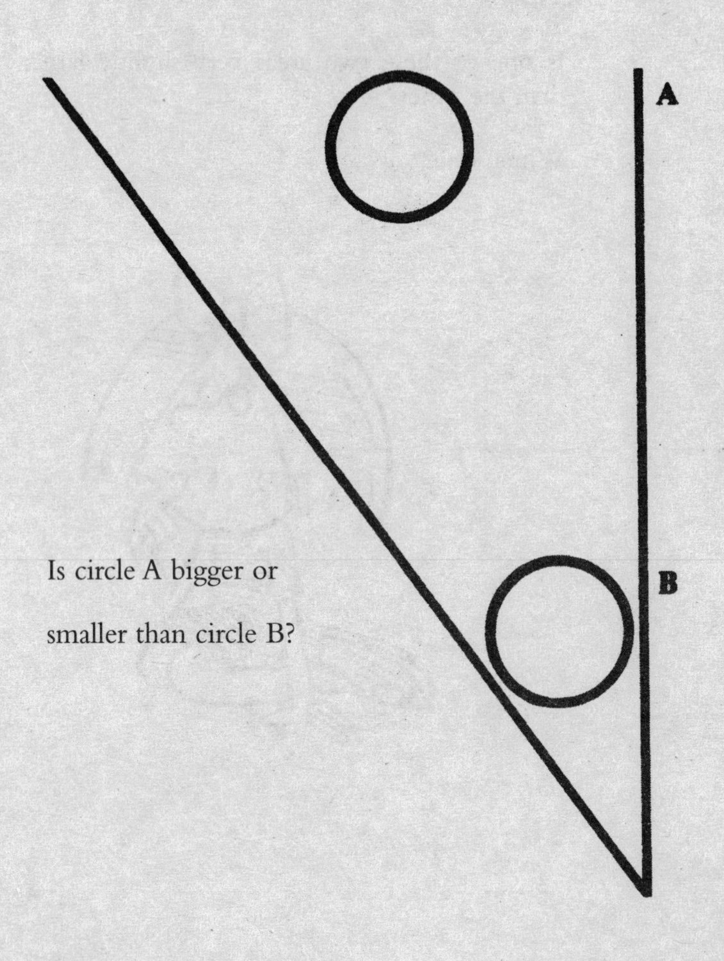

Is circle A bigger or smaller than circle B?

Both the circles are the same size. If they look different, it is because of their positions inside the angle.

Square World

Is one of these two areas very slightly larger than the other?

Which one?

The white square seems a little larger than the black square, but in fact they're both exactly the same size.

31

Watch 'em Bend!

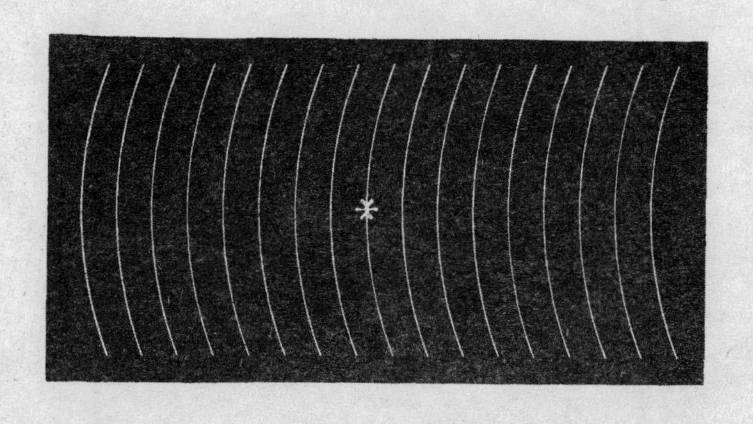

Look at the star on this page steadily while you count to 100 very slowly.

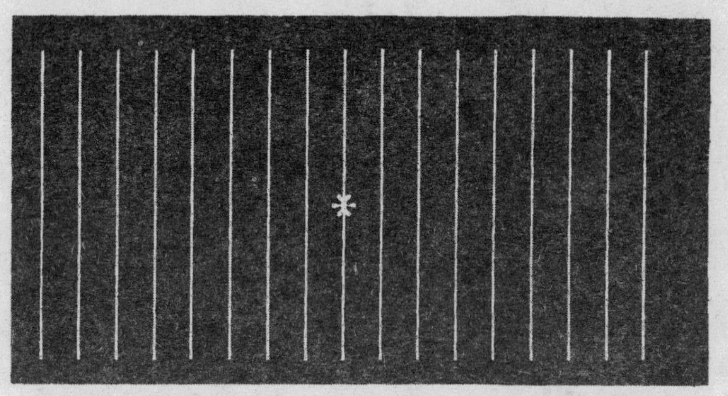

Now look at the star
on *this* page and watch
the lines curve in the
opposite direction!

Impossible!

Look at the opposite page.

Whichever way you look at it, this is an "impossible" object.

That is, it is possible to *draw* it on paper, but you could never *build* it out of cardboard or wood.

If it looks perfectly all right to you, look again—starting at the base of the object and then letting your eye move up it.

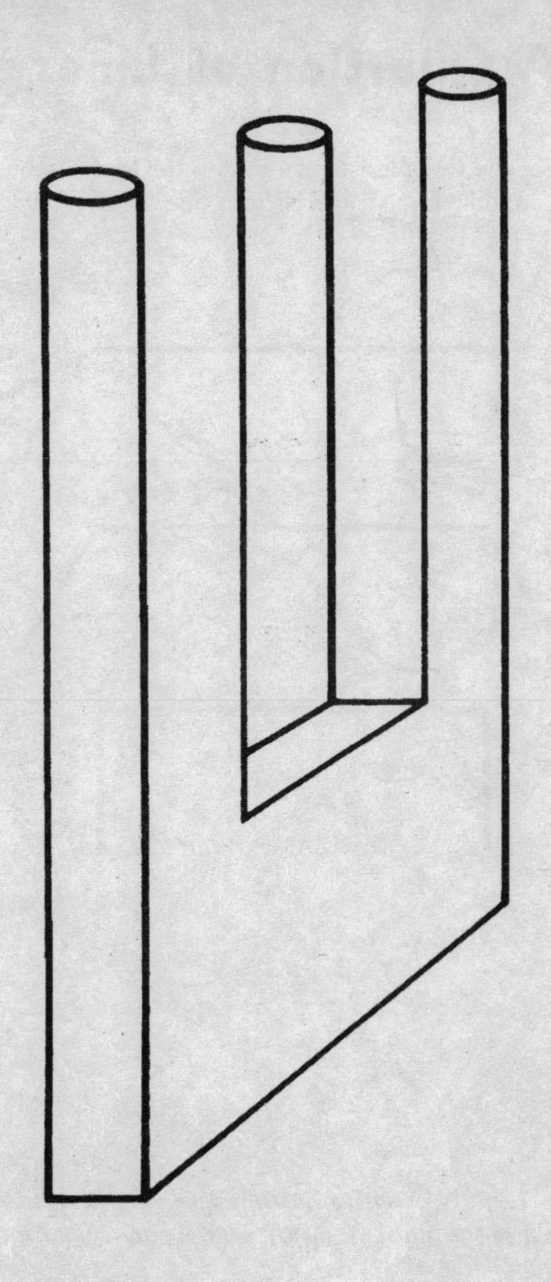

35

A Question of Lines

Which of the three horizontal lines is the longest: the top one, the middle one, or the bottom one?

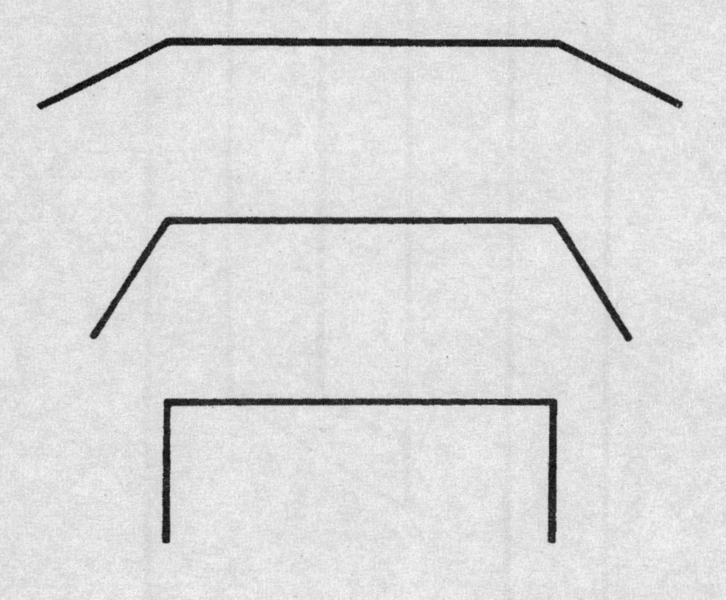

All three lines are the same length. It is the angles that make the horizontal lines look different lengths.

A Questions of Angles

Which is the longer line:
the one from A to C
or
the one from B to D?

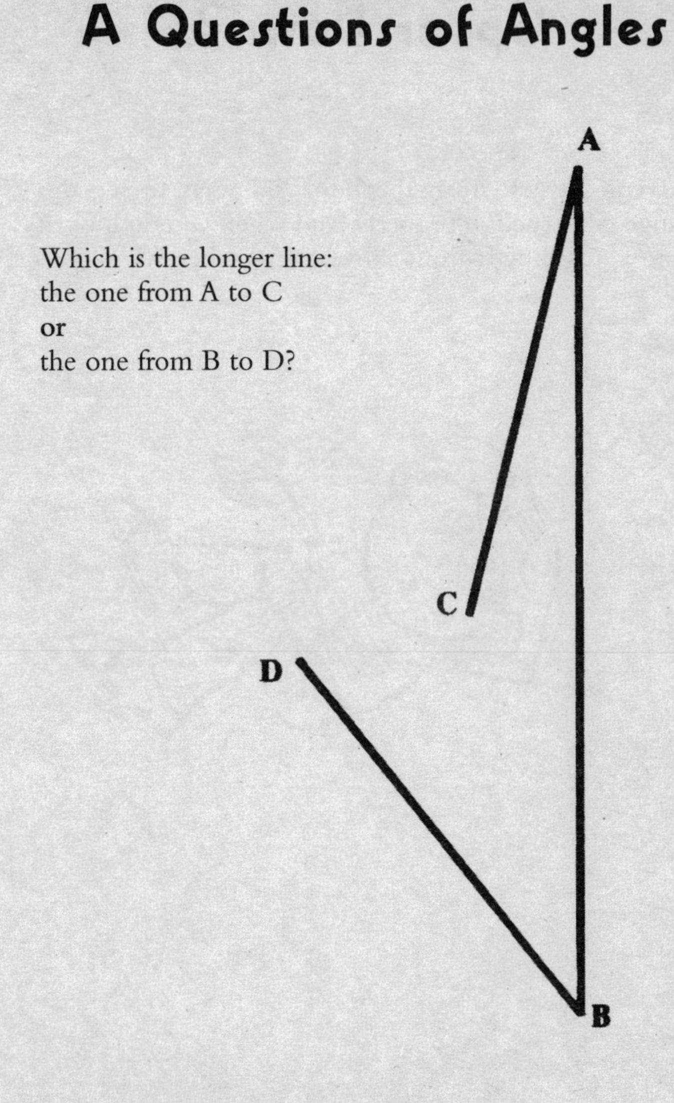

Both lines are the same length. It is the angles the lines make that cause them to look different.

Up or Down?

You will have to turn the book sideways to see this strange construction properly. And when you do look at it, are you seeing it from above or from below?

This is one of those odd figures that you feel you are seeing from above at one moment and from below at the next. Whichever way you look at it, it's still confusing!

Thick and Thin

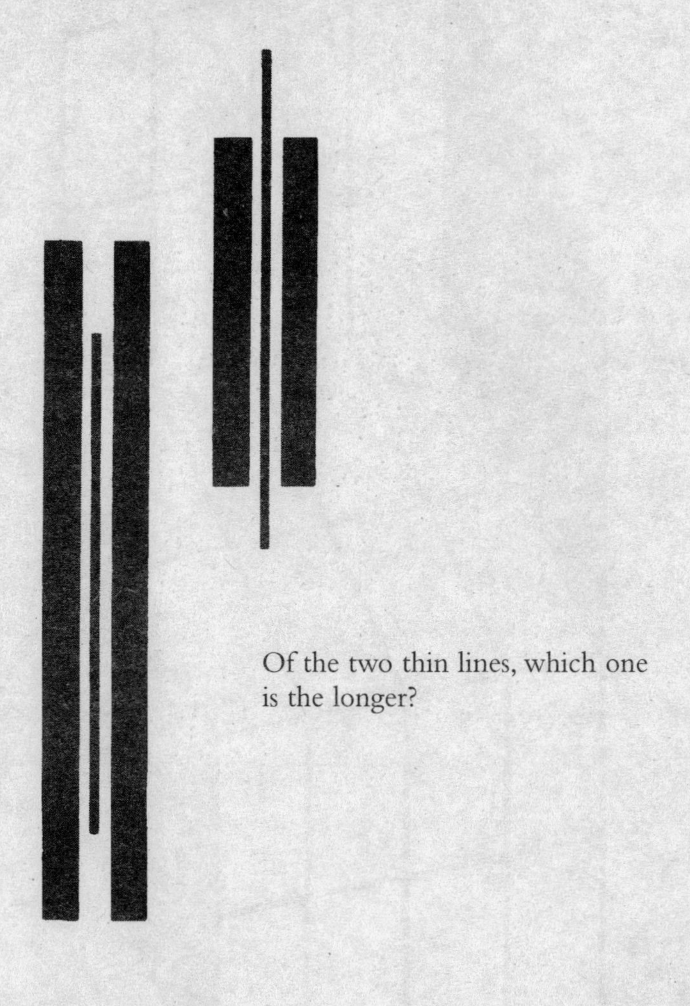

Of the two thin lines, which one is the longer?

The two thin lines are of equal lengths. They look different because of the different lengths of thick lines on either side of them.

Wooden Triangle

If you're any good at carpentry, try making this simple wooden triangle.

Actually, you can't do it! The wooden triangle is one of those "impossible objects" that are easy to draw, but not to make.

Bull's-Eye

Revolve the pages and the spirals will seem to get bigger or smaller depending upon in which direction you are turning the book.

Center Point

Glance at the facing page and tell what you can see right in the very middle of it.

If you said you saw the letter B that's because you first perceived the horizontal line of letters A, B, C. If you said you saw the number 13 that's because you first perceived the vertical line of numbers 12, 13, 14.

12

A B C

14

Master Carpenter

Ask a friend if he can build this hollow crate for you from 12 pieces of wood. Tell him he can save $1000 if he succeeds!

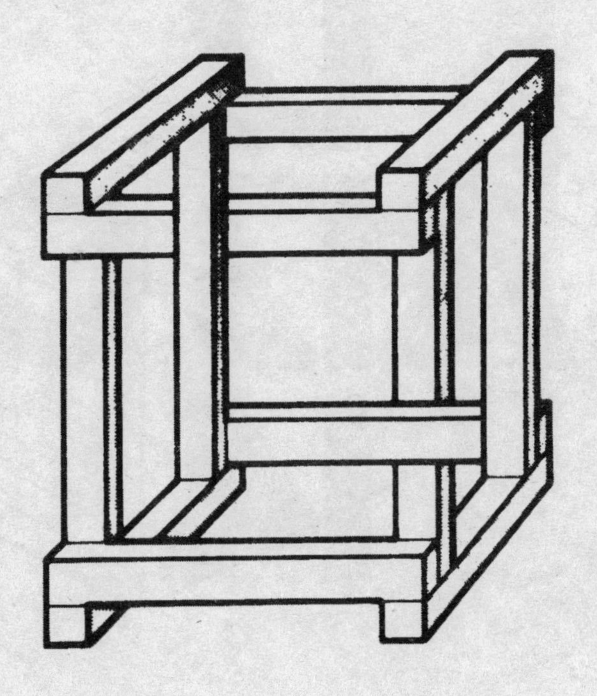

Don't worry, your money's safe. No matter how skilled a carpenter your friend happens to be, he'll never be able to build the crate. It's an impossible object.

Upstairs Downstairs

Find the top step. When (and **if**) you find it, start looking for the bottom step!

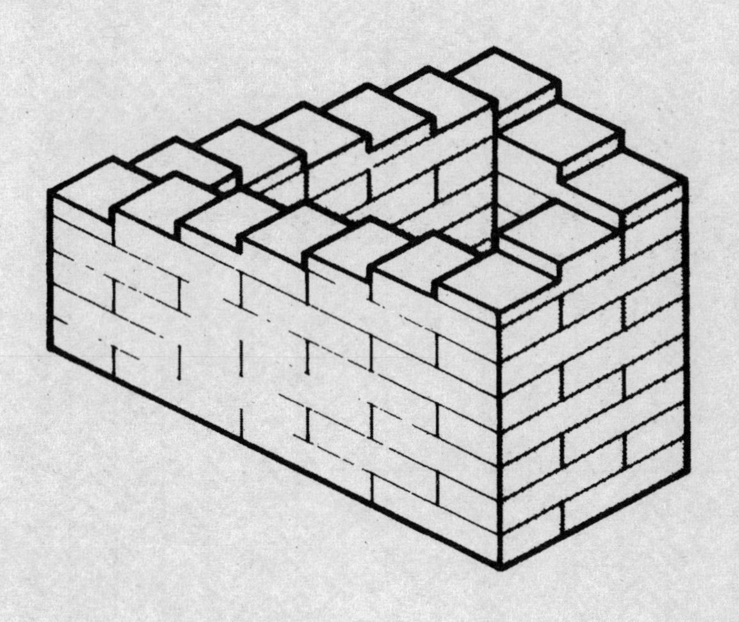

If you think you managed to find the top and bottom steps, you're wrong! They don't exist because the stairway is an impossibility!

Straight and Narrow

How many of the vertical lines on the facing page are bending this way and that? And how many of them are perfectly straight?

They are all perfectly straight. It is the pattern of wavy lines behind them that makes them appear to bend.

How Far This Time?

A

B

Is the distance between A and B greater or smaller than the distance between C and D?

C

D

It looks greater, but in fact it's the same.

Strange Circles

Which of the three rings is a perfect circle?

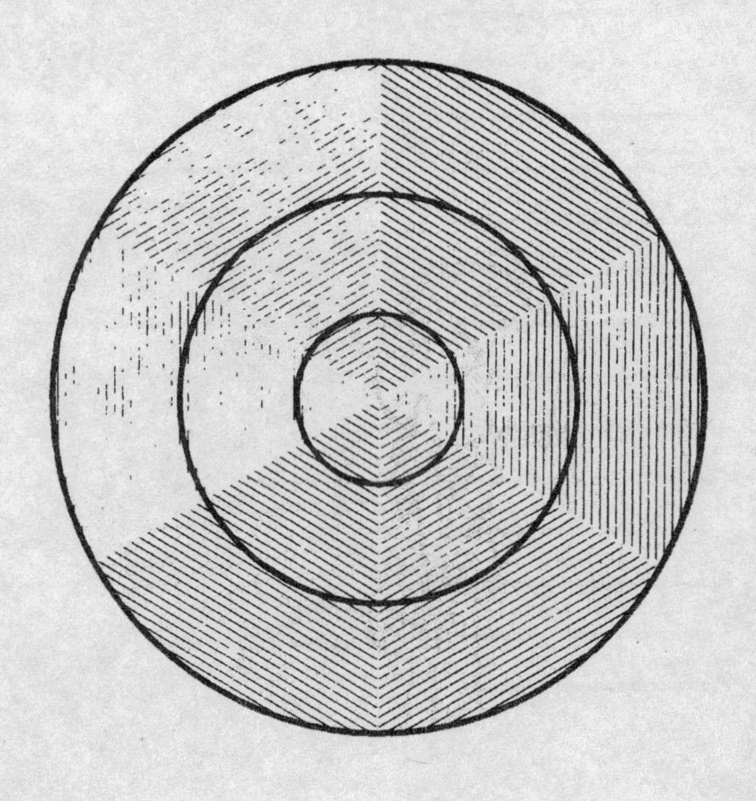

All three are! It is the background pattern that makes the perfect circles seem distorted.

Some Circles

Of the two center circles, which one is the bigger?

They are both the same size. The top one only looks bigger because it is surrounded by smaller circles and the bottom one only looks smaller because it is surrounded by bigger circles.

Point of View

Look carefully at the two horizontal lines.

Which one is longer: the top one or the bottom one?

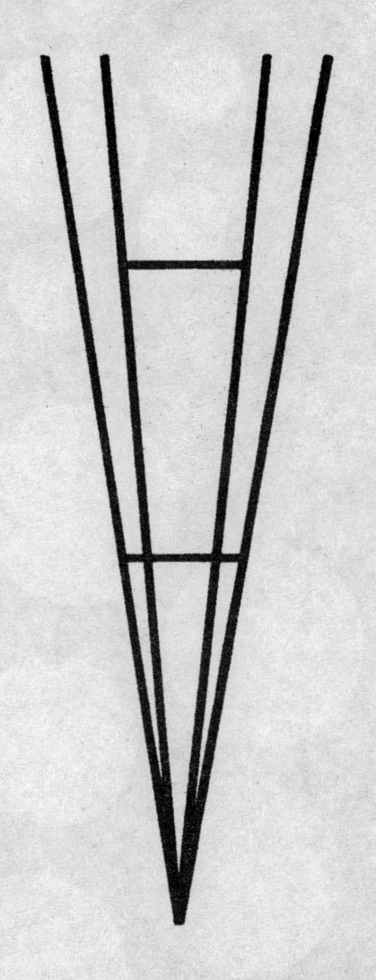

Both are exactly the same length. It's the difference in position that makes the lower one look longer.

A Curve Ball

Which of the three arcs is the biggest:

the top one,

the middle one,

or the bottom one?

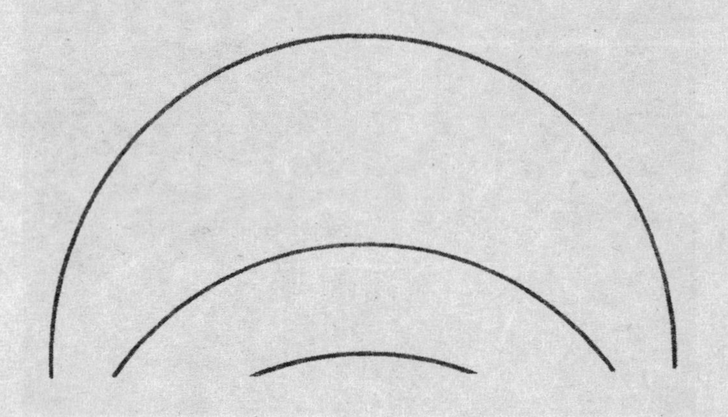

All three are arcs from exactly the same circle, but the more you see of each arc the greater the curve seems to be.

The Long and Short of It

Which of the two horizontal lines is the longer? It looks like the top one, but are you **sure**?

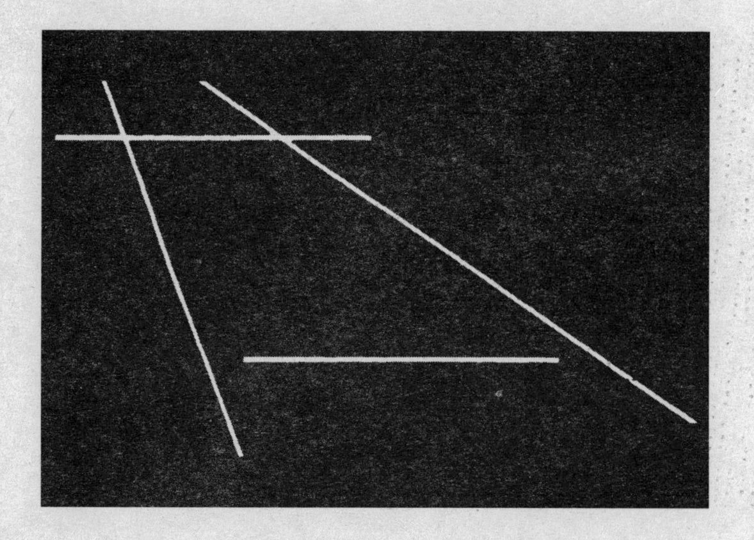

Both the horizontal lines are the same length. It's the converging lines that make the top line look longer.

Square Dance

Why does each side of the square bend inward slightly in the middle?

In fact, it's a perfect square. The sides don't bend at all. They just seem to because of the pattern of rings behind.

In or Out?

Look carefully at the two vertical lines on the opposite page.

Do they bend inward at the middle?

Do they bend outward at the middle?

Are they perfectly straight?

The lines look as if they bend inwards at the middle, but they don't. They are perfectly straight parallel lines.

From Here to There

Is the line from A to B longer or shorter than the line from C to D?

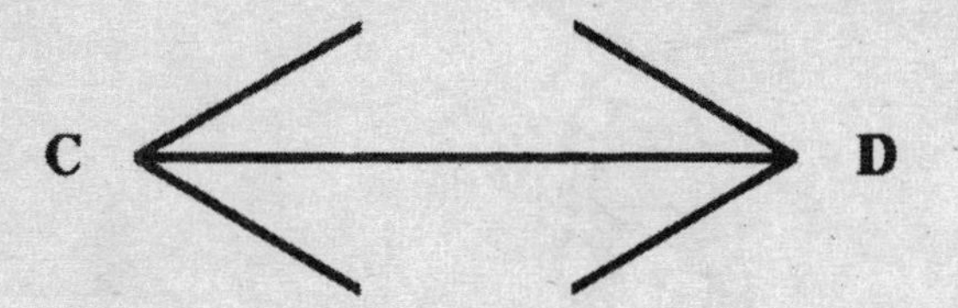

It looks longer, but both lines are actually the same length.

Where Are You?

Are you up in the sky looking down on the roof of a house? Or are you in a room looking into a corner?

The answer is either! The line in the middle will either appear nearer to you (the roof) or farther away from you (the corner)—depending on how you see it!

Which End Is Up?

Here's an unusual tube. Look carefully at it for at least a minute and then decide if you are looking down the tube from above it or up the tube from under it.

You can look at the tube either way. Sometimes you'll feel you're seeing through it from the top and sometimes from the bottom!

Great or Small?

Which of the two circles is the larger?

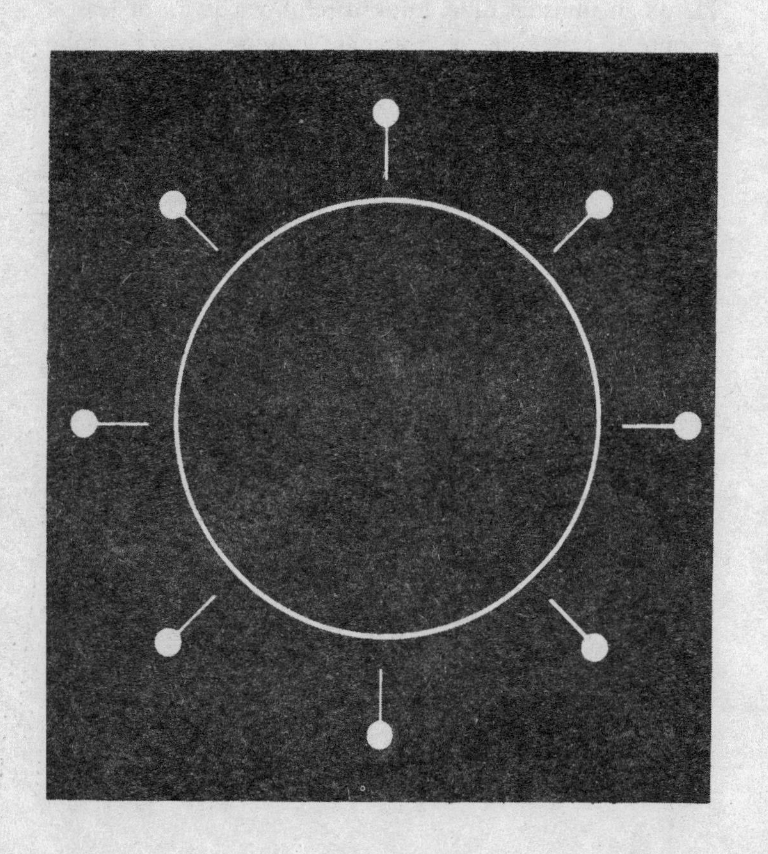

The one on this page?

You may be wrong! The one on this page certainly looks smaller, but in fact both circles are identical in size.

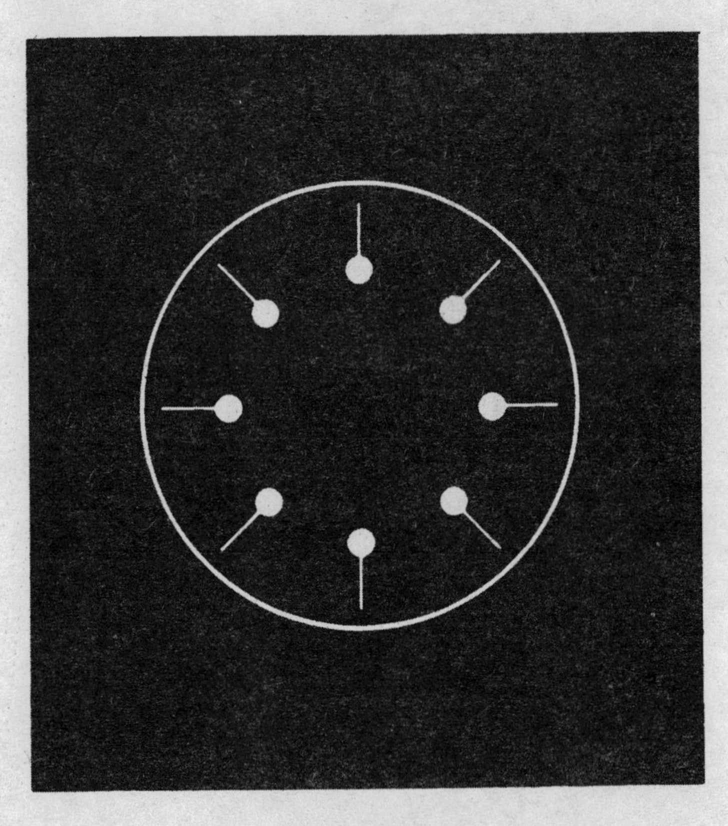

Or the one on this page?

Crisscross

Glance at the facing page and strange gray spots will appear at all the points where the lines cross. Look at any one crossing in particular and the gray spot that was there will suddenly disappear!

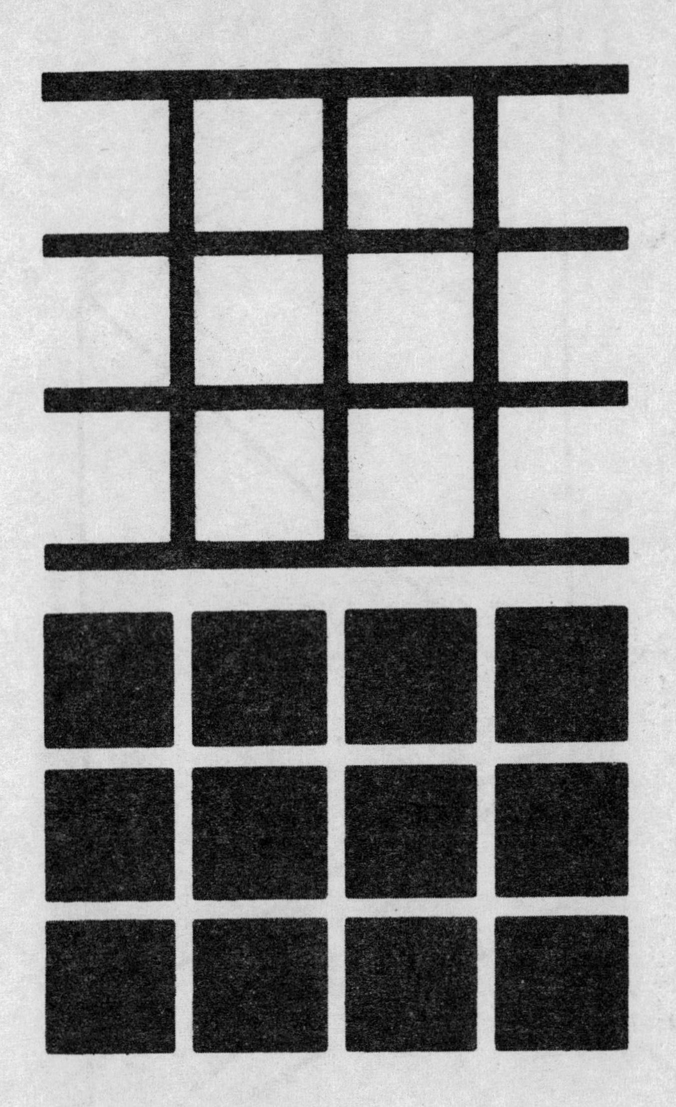

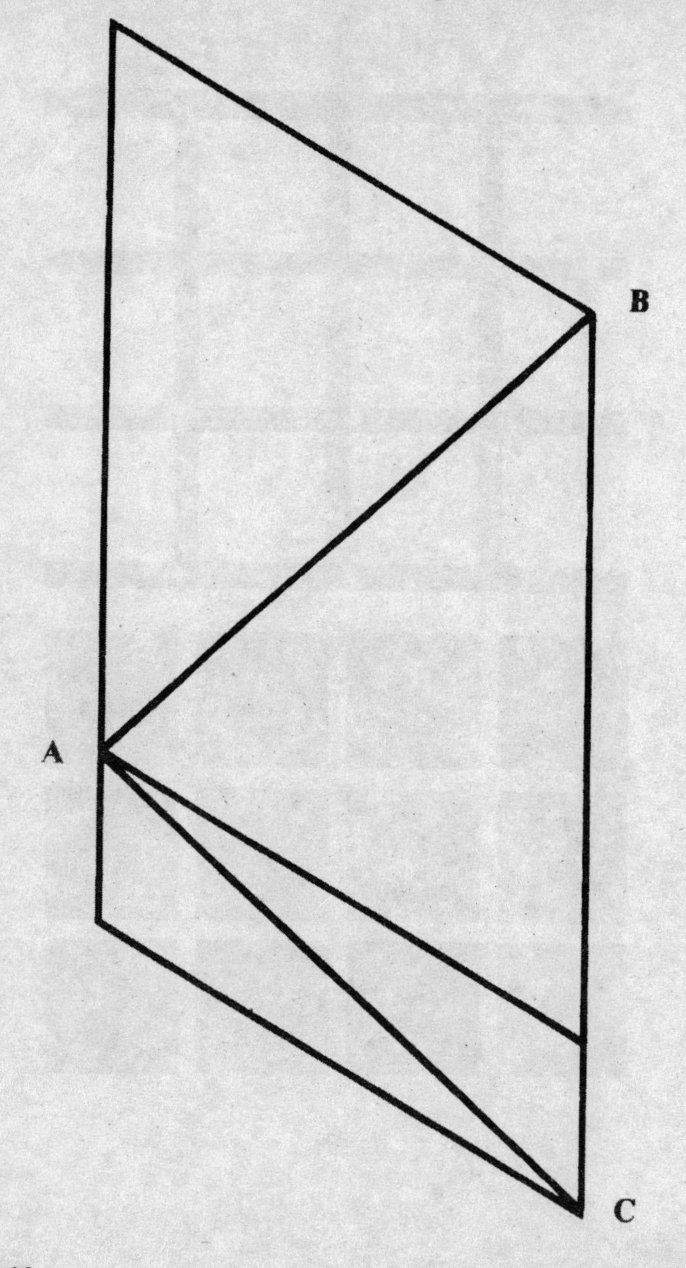

68

69

AB looks a lot longer, but in fact both lines are the same length. Check with a ruler if you don't believe us.

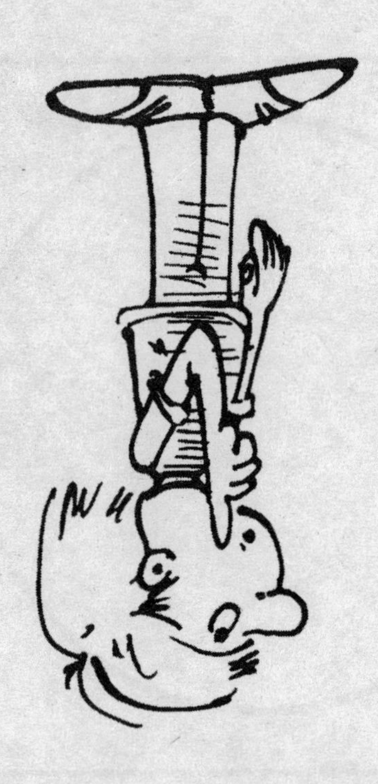

Which line is longer: AB or AC?

Look carefully at the parallelogram opposite.

Parallel Bars

Square Circles

Which of the two circles is the larger?

A

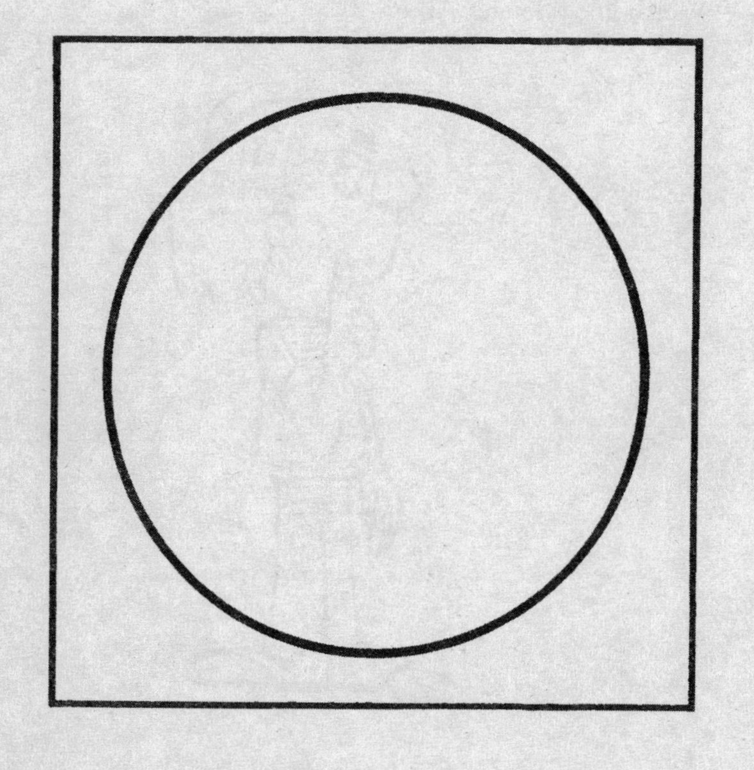

A looks a little larger than B, but in fact both the circles are the same size. It's the position and size of the boxes that deceive you.

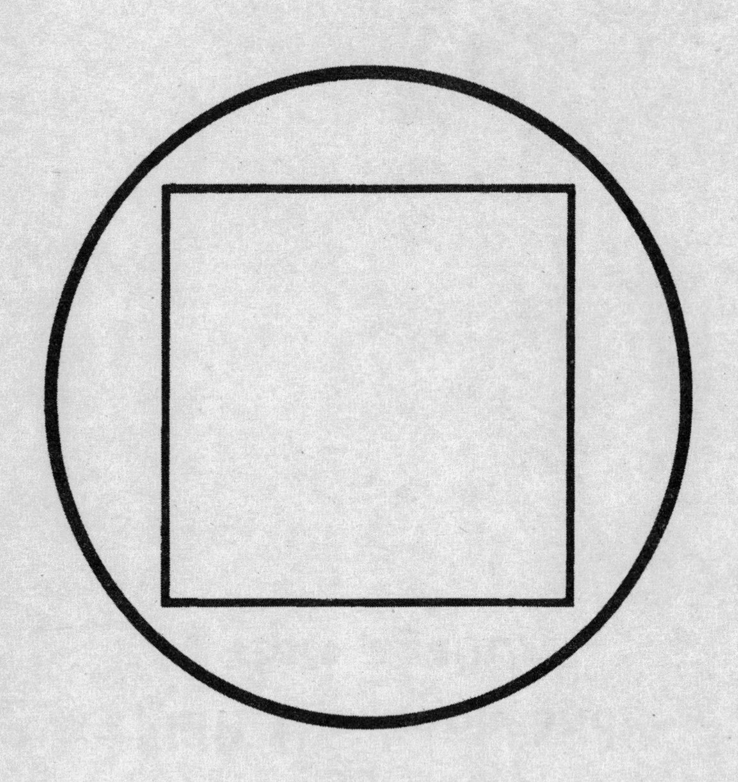

B

Now are your eyes boggled? FLIP the book and start again!